FRACTURED
SOUL

FRACTURED SOUL

A NOVEL

AKIRA MIZUBAYASHI

Translated by ALISON ANDERSON

HarperVia

An Imprint of HarperCollinsPublishers

Excerpt from *Moments musicaux* by Theodor W. Adorno, English translation © Wieland Hoban, 2009.

Excerpts from String Quartet no. 13 in A Minor, D. 804, op. 29, *Rosamunde*, by Franz Schubert. Photo © IMSLP/CC.BY SA 4.0.

HarperCollins books may be purchased for educational, business, or sales promotional use. For information, please email the Special Markets Department at SPsales@harpercollins.com.

Originally published as *Âme brisée* in France in 2019 by Éditions Gallimard.

FIRST HARPERVIA EDITION PUBLISHED IN 2023

Designed by Janet Evans Scanlon
Illustrations © Nattha99/stock.adobe.com

Library of Congress Cataloging-in-Publication Data is available upon request.

ISBN 978-0-06-309366-9

23 24 25 26 27 LBC 5 4 3 2 1

To all the ghosts in the world

SOUND POST or SOUL POST, noun. *Music. The sound post of a stringed instrument.* Little wooden dowel inserted into the body of the instrument, between the top plate and back plate, to maintain them at the proper distance and ensure the quality, resonance, and uniformity of the vibrations.

Treasures of the English Language

In the face of Schubert's music, the tear falls from the eye without first asking the soul: it falls into us, so remote from all images and so real. We weep without knowing why; because we have not yet reached the state promised by the music and, in our unspoken joy, all we need is for it to assure us that we one day will.

Theodor W. Adorno, *Moments musicaux*

PAUSE FOR CONTEMPLATION

Sunday, November 6, 1938, Tokyo

"The sharp clip of approaching boots, getting louder, slowing. Someone walking. Stopped. Started. Stopped again. Now he's very near. I think I can hear him breathing. A faint sound of something brushing wood. Has he just set something down on the bench? I'm in the dark, trembling with fear. It sends a chill down my spine. Silence. Suddenly, the darkness is lifted. A large luminous square opens before me. What can I see? My eyes, dazzled, see the tall body of a man, severely upright, uniformed in khaki. I can't see his head or his feet. I can see the front of his uniform, buttons neatly aligned along the vertical, a heavy saber dangling from his waist, his arms, his hands emerging from his sleeves, both legs like sturdy tree trunks down to the knees. The light cruelly exposes my feet in their green cotton socks; I can't hide them any better. Next to my petrified feet, my book . . . its white cover edged with a thin orange stripe. The title in thick black characters shamelessly offers itself to the bright light: *How Do You Live?* Below, in small characters, the author's name is printed, and at the bottom, medium-size, the name of the book's collection: The Little Citizens' Library. Is he going to take it? Hurry up, you have to beat him to it! No, it's better if I don't move . . . A fraction of a second later I place my right hand on the book and pick it up. But I slowly move my trembling hand away . . . Several endless seconds go by. I don't know what he's doing—his body hasn't moved an inch. I'm afraid. Instinctively, I close my eyes. The silence lingers. I open my eyes halfway. Now he bends forward, slowly, very slowly, as if hesitating, as if unsure of what he's doing. A man's head, wearing a field cap that matches his uniform, appears before my eyes. Backlit, obscured by deep shadow. At the back of the cap, a piece of khaki cloth hangs down to his shoulders. His eyes alone are shining, like a cat lurking in the half-light. My eyes, now wide open, meet his. I think I can make out the beginnings of a faint smile, spreading to his eyes. What is he going to do? Is he going to hurt me? Is he going to force me out of hiding? I withdraw even farther. He abruptly leans to one side and bends over, then immediately stands up, the ruined violin in hand; that must be what he placed on the bench a few seconds ago, just beside the wardrobe where I am hiding. Suddenly a man's voice can be heard, loud and urgent, quickly approaching: 'Kurokami! Kurokami!'

"Mechanically, he cocks his head as if wondering where, exactly, the voice is coming from, as if he's trying to identify the person shouting, all the while his face contracting with tension.

"Without a word, he hands me the broken violin, almost flat, its four strings forming a warped contour; in the dark it looks like a little dying animal. I don't know what to do. I hesitate, but in the end I take the damaged instrument, timidly, into both hands.

"'Kurokami! Lieutenant Kurokami!'

"He hurries to close the door, after glancing at me one last time. The worried, distraught look he flashes is followed by the ghost of a smile—quickly erased as the man who's been shouting his name approaches.

"'Oh, there you are! What on earth are you doing here, Kurokami? We're leaving. No time to mess around.'

"'Yes, sir! Forgive me, I was just making sure we hadn't overlooked anything.'

"In the darkness of the wardrobe I can distinctly hear the hard male voice I think belongs to the man who was shouting 'Kurokami!' I'm surprised to hear the name Kurokami, because I never dreamed a last name could mean 'black hair.' The man is saying something I can't grasp very well; his tone is commanding, or like that of someone who is very angry. He frightens me. Another male voice replies quite calmly, evenly, almost gently. Is that the voice of the man who gave me the violin?

"Gradually the voices recede. The footsteps, too. I remain in darkness. Before long I can't hear anything. Or rather, at the periphery of my ears I hear something like the faint, stubborn trill of dying cicadas. It's tinnitus, a word I learned from my father not long ago. In a way, it's the sound of silence. I peer through the keyhole. The room is dark because the black curtains have been drawn, but there's enough light from the neons to convince me no one is here anymore. What time is it? Night hasn't fallen yet, but I'm starting to get hungry. I listen . . . and convince myself that really, no one is here anymore. So, I lift the latch as quietly as possible, trying not to make the slightest noise as I open the door. But it creaks. 'Shut up!' I think. I wait a little. Nothing new—it's still as silent. There's no one here anymore. I put my canvas shoes back on—I'd taken them off, to not make any noise. I leave my hiding place, the broken violin in my hands and my book in the pocket of my trousers. I take a few timid steps; I'm having trouble walking: Ah! My legs have gone to sleep! I stop. I wait a few seconds. I start walking again. I cross the big hall and go toward the door. With all my weight I push the heavy entrance door. Now I'm standing outside the municipal cultural center. I look up at the sky. Day is departing. It's starting to get dark. I feel helpless and alone. Sobs catch in my throat. A huge black force is crushing me, projecting shapeless suffocating shadows onto me. People walk by in the street. Soldiers from the military police, with rifles on their shoulders, are on patrol. I can't see a single child around. Where has Papa gone? Will he come back? Or go straight home? I start down the street that leads home. I hurry my steps . . . cradling the ruined violin as if it were a dying animal I must save at all costs."

I'm standing rooted at the altar of the wide-open cupboard. My eyes are closed. I can smell behind me the sweet perfume of a female presence. I step slowly down the dark stairway of time . . .

I

ALLEGRO MA NON TROPPO

1

.

IT WAS A SUNDAY AFTERNOON OF MEEK SUNLIGHT. THE ELEVEN-year-old schoolboy was reading all alone on a bench with a backrest in the meeting hall of the municipal cultural center. He was immersed in his book. It looked as though nothing could distract him from the pages he was turning at regular intervals, so mesmerized was he by the story he read, by the words he savored, as motionless as a statue. As for his father, he wore a simple gray jacket, while he swept the floor that was scattered here and there with bits of fluff. Once he finished his summary housekeeping, he set up, side by side, two folding music stands he'd brought from home.

"Well then, Rei, is Coper's story interesting?"

Rei didn't budge. Coper, a nickname for Copernicus, was the protagonist of his book: a fifteen-year-old Japanese school-boy. In fact, they called him Coper-kun, adding the suffix for familiarity.

"While we're rehearsing, you can go on reading, but you must say hello when they arrive! You hear me?"

"Yes, Papa."

The boy replied in a low voice, swallowing a bit of air, never tearing his eyes from the page. His father headed toward the entrance hall. Only seconds after vanishing down the corridor, he returned with two big empty cardboard boxes meant for transporting fruit, one brown, the other yellow, clementines drawn on their sides. He placed them vertically, first one, then the other, so that they stood on either side of the metal music stands. The father turned to his son.

"How far are you?"

The boy didn't answer.

His father raised his voice.

"Hey! Rei, where are you in the book?"

"Oh, I'm sorry, Papa, uh, I'm at the statues of Buddha in Gan . . . dha . . . ra . . ." Rei stumbled over the word *Gandhara*.

"Ah, that's where the uncle explains that it was the Greeks who came up with making statues of Buddha, long before people in Asia. That's a terrific passage!"

"I've nearly finished, it's such a pity!" murmured Rei, fingering the thin layer of pages he had left.

"So, it didn't make you cry?"

"Oh, it did, when Kitami-kun defends Urakawa-kun from Yamaguchi. Everyone makes fun of him, the poor boy!"

"When Yamaguchi and his gang ridicule Urakawa-kun for the fried tofu he has in his bento every day, since his parents are tofu merchants. You mean there?"

"Yes. Then there's another scene: Coper hasn't got the courage to side with his two friends. The gang of older boys bullies them! I didn't cry, but I was infuriated by those arrogant older boys! They tell Kitami-kun to obey. Otherwise, others will think he doesn't like his school, that he's a traitor!"

"Ah yes, that scene is thrilling. But didn't you like what came next? There are some beautiful pages about Coper suffering precisely because of his cowardice. Then his mother is so kind to her son. You know, Coper's mother reminds me of your mother."

"Yes, yes, when his mother tells him about things she couldn't do because she was too shy, or when she lacked courage, regarding the old lady climbing the steps to a temple with a big bundle. That made me cry. Coper's father died, and with me it's my mother . . . So, we're similar . . ."

"You know, Rei, I'd like for the two of us to discuss this book, once you've finished."

Rei, already lost in the final pages, didn't respond.

Just then, steps were heard in the entrance hall. A man in his forties, rather tall, with blond hair, came into the big hall. He wore a beige suit with a blue cotton scarf around his neck.

"Hello, Yu. How are you? I thought I'd find you here. You said you'd be rehearsing with your musician friends this afternoon."

"Ah! Hello, Philippe! What a surprise! What brings you here? I didn't expect to see you," said Yu, his French somewhat hesitant but fluent.

"Um . . ."

"You seem worried, Philippe."

Over Yu's shoulder the foreign visitor noticed the boy gazing somewhat dreamily from his book at the two adults conversing.

"How are you, Rei? What are you reading?" asked Philippe, in Japanese that was perfectly comprehensible, despite his strange intonation. Philippe, not waiting for a reply, looked Yu in the eyes. "My wife and I have decided to go back to France. Life is becoming difficult for me here. I've asked to be repatriated. The newspaper's decision should come any day now. Anyway,

I would have liked to talk about all that with you, but it looks like just now you won't have time."

Yu looked at his watch. "No, they'll be here any minute. Can you stop by my place this evening? Or I can come and see you, if you like. Otherwise tomorrow evening, if that works for you."

"All right, I'll come to your place tonight, but it will be rather late, around eight o'clock, eight thirty, if it's not a bother," said Philippe, after hesitating for a moment.

The people Yu was expecting had just come into the hall. Two men and a woman, between twenty-five and thirty years of age. Yu greeted them with a bow and shook their hands. Afterward, he introduced Philippe, adding that he was a correspondent for a French newspaper. Yu's friends were Chinese. The youngest of the three was named Kang. In his left hand he carried a violin in its case. The young woman, called Yanfen, was a viola player, and her case was slightly bigger. The last visitor, who looked older than the others, with his beard and receding hairline, was bravely carrying a cello case on his shoulders. His name was Cheng. The three amateurs were among the few Chinese students who'd not conformed to a narrow-minded nationalism, exacerbated by the animosity between the Middle Kingdom and the Japanese Empire. Since the 1931 Manchurian Incident, colonial expansionism had been gaining ground.

"Mizusawa-san, perhaps you're busy today?" said Cheng to Yu in fluent Japanese, a smile blooming on his wide face.

Yu noticed that Cheng was glancing furtively at his journalist friend.

"No, don't worry, Cheng-san, I'm all yours. Philippe-san and I will have all the time we need later on." Just as Cheng had done with his family name, Mizusawa, Yu added the affectionate suffix to each of their names.

"I'll stay and listen for a while. Don't pay me any mind, Yu."

"Thank you, Philippe. See you this evening."

"Yes."

Yu went over to a storage room beside the bench. He took out two stools, and on his way back said to his son, lost to the outside world, "Rei, they're here now. Go say hello!"

His son stood up and looked at his father's three Chinese friends, who were taking out their instruments.

"Konnichiwa!" said Rei in a clear voice, making little bows.

The Chinese musicians answered him at the same time. The men raised their hands in greeting, while Yanfen gave him a lovely smile and told him she was curious to find out about the book keeping him so thoroughly engrossed. Rei was surprised by the velvety beauty of her voice and by the Japanese words she uttered in an uninterrupted flow. He looked at the young woman. She was wearing a dark brown dress that enhanced the smooth lines of her slender body. Her oval face shone a brilliant white. Her shoulder-length black hair was tied behind her bare neck. Her eyes were like a spill of jewels reflecting a gentle ray of morning sun from every angle. She wore no lipstick, and her lips moved like leaves quivering to the whim of a warm spring breeze. To finish the drawing, a mysterious curved line ran from her chin down to the faint roundness of her breasts.

Surprised by the indiscretion of his eyes, Rei tried to contain himself, quickly returning his gaze to his book, but his diverted attention could no longer find the beginning of the lines.

Yu set the stools down in front of the music stands. Kang returned from the storage room with two more stools, which he put next to the cardboard boxes. Yu in turn took his violin out of its case, which he had left on the floor between the bench and a tall European wardrobe of carved mahogany, its looming presence simultaneously mammoth yet discreet. Then without thinking he went to put the case away in the storage room.

Now all four of them were sitting in a semicircle. Yu played first violin; Kang, second. Next to Kang sat Yanfen with her viola. Finally, Cheng, the cellist, sat almost directly across from Yu, six feet away. Once they had placed their respective scores on either box or music stand, they began to tune their instruments. Suddenly Yu turned to speak to his son, as if he had just remembered something important.

"Excuse me, Rei, could you draw the black curtains and switch on the light?"

This time Rei reacted immediately.

"This is our third session, but we still haven't progressed any further than the first movement!" said Yu, speaking to Philippe in French. Then he hurriedly translated the exclamation into Japanese for his Chinese friends.

"Fortunately! We're trying to prolong the pleasure as much as we can," said Cheng with a laugh. "We're in no hurry, are we?"

They all laughed wholeheartedly. Philippe joined in, encouraged by their good humor, but he thought he could sense the tiniest trace of poorly hidden anxiety.

"Ready?" said Yu to the other musicians.

There was a long silence. Then with a slight nod, Kang signaled to the viola player and the cellist to start, while Yu, propping his instrument beneath his chin, where it gleamed in the dim light from the neon overhead, waited to make his entrance, his bow still in the air. Pianissimo, Kang played a languorous melody that slipped gently over the regular lapping of bass notes provided by Yanfen and Cheng.

Philippe, who was more than a mere music lover, having played the clarinet since adolescence, immediately recognized the opening of Schubert's String Quartet in A Minor, opus 29, *Rosamunde*. Dazzled by the tremulous beauty of music he had not heard in a long time, he sat motionless for several minutes on the bench beside Rei. The boy held his book open while staring at his father, who was totally absorbed by the open pages of the musical score. But after a glance at his pocket watch, Philippe slowly got up. He placed his hand delicately on Rei's head and whispered, "Mata ne!" *Bye-bye!* Then he went to the door on tiptoe, not looking at the musicians as they played. Before closing the door, however, for a split second Philippe trained his intense, penetrating gaze on Yu, who responded with a barely perceptible smile. As for the three Chinese musicians, they were focused on their score, and the discreet departure of the French journalist did not disturb them, while the schoolboy Rei was already lost in his book again.

2.

THE SINO-JAPANESE QUARTET, ONLY RECENTLY ESTABLISHED, DID not have a name. It was founded on the sole precept of a shared pleasure in music, beyond any other considerations; it was oblivious to anything that was not Schubert, and was at a remove from the rest of the world, in order to listen to itself and to others. The four members had now begun, note by note, to explore the first movement of *Rosamunde*. The execution of this monumental movement required roughly a quarter of an hour. They'd been working on it fervently for nearly half an hour but still had not reached the end of their troubles—far from it. They'd finished practicing the repeat. And yet they did not feel ready to go on and attack the seconda volta. Yanfen suggested they commence again from the beginning and pause whenever they felt something wasn't working. "What do you think?"

On hearing the female voice Rei, still immersed in his book, raised his head to glance at the young woman. He wondered why and how she could speak so *fluently*, without any accent, like a proper Japanese woman. She spoke so naturally, with such grace, that she aroused in him a feeling of astonishment intermingled with admiration.

"I'd like to start again at the beginning, too," said Kang, timidly. "I'm not at all satisfied with my exposition . . ."

"The viola and the cello provide the base of the construction with this particular rhythm," said Cheng. "Tah . . . takatakata . . . tah . . . takatakata . . . tah . . . takatakata . . . I get the impression we're not completely together, in unison with Kang-san."

When Cheng was discussing something in Japanese with Kang and Yanfen, he frequently added the suffix *san* to their first names. He liked the civility and friendly sense of egalitarianism it seemed to convey.

"Yes, that's it," answered Yanfen. "We have to aim for a certain harmony and fullness, I think, sonically. If our foundations aren't solid, the first violin won't be able to impose the main theme, which is absolutely magnificent."

"You're right, Yanfen-san," said Yu in turn.

He then went on speaking slowly, as if thinking out loud, bringing carefully selected words to his lips.

"I think we have to agree on the tempo to adopt. Schubert indicated *allegro ma non troppo*. In my opinion, it must be slow enough to convey a certain gravity, a gravity inherent in the work, but not too much, precisely in order to avoid lapsing into an excess of sentimentality."

"We played it too quickly," murmured Cheng, looking at Yanfen.

"Yes, I think we did," said Yu.

Then he went on. "The theme I'm going to play is, in my opinion, an expression of nostalgia for a bygone world, which might be mixed with childhood. In any case, it's a world of peace and serenity, more harmonious than today's world with its ugliness and violence. On the other hand, I see the motif played by the viola and the cello—the tah . . . takatakata . . .

tah . . . takatakata—as the obstinate presence of danger about to invade this apparently untroubled life. The melody Kang-san introduces translates the frightening sadness that lies deep in our hearts . . ."

"Oh, you put that very well, Mizusawa-san!" said Kang.

The young Chinese musician thought Yu's expression rendered perfectly his own feelings regarding the initial motif he was responsible for. "Frightening sadness" did not leave Yanfen indifferent, either; a melody had been coming back to her, obsessively: that of the extraordinary piano accompaniment to the *Erlkönig*. But she refrained from mentioning it.

"So, we start over?" suggested Cheng.

The four musicians prepared to attack the beginning of the first movement again. After a long silence of several seconds, Kang at last gave a slight nod, the signal to start. Supported by the frightening little rhythmic tremors, executed more slowly by the viola and cello, led by the second violin's supple, fluid mediant, Schubert's soundscape now seemed more obviously colored with unspeakable sadness.

"Do-mi-do-ti-do-mi-la-mi, do-mi-do-ti-do-mi-la-mi."

Here Yu slipped gently into the music, placing his notes onto the foundation of sound, constructed pianissimo but solidly by the other instruments: a sovereign exposition of the hauntingly beautiful first theme.

"Mi~~~do~la~~,do~ti~~~~-re-do-ti-do-ti-la-~do~ti~~~sol#~ do~~~la~re~~re#~~mi~~~."

Yu was playing with his eyes closed, as if his inner concentration, detached from all the world around him, helped him enter as deeply as possible into the essence of the sound. When he had finished exposing the theme, he opened his eyes and, smiling, intimated to his teammates to keep up the momentum and carry on.

Thus the quartet played the entire opening of the first movement in one go, and when they were about to start the seconda volta, the four musicians paused naturally, as if they had agreed ahead of time.

"I think that was much better," Kang said timidly.

"Yes, I think that was very good. I'm getting so much pleasure from participating in this shared endeavor!" said Yanfen enthusiastically, her face reddening slightly.

"I didn't do a very good job with the theme at the point where it shifts to major," said Yu, scratching his head with his right hand, no longer holding the bow.

"Yes, you did, it wasn't bad, Mizusawa-san," Kang hurriedly said.

"It's a moment of transcendent beauty! And I didn't measure up, I don't think . . ."

"It's true it's magnificent, the way the tonality changes," said Cheng. "It's as if the landscape were suddenly illuminated, if only for a moment . . ."

The quartet continued in this manner for another hour or so, until somehow they finished playing the entire first movement. When the first violin repeated the great, melancholy theme over the last twenty bars, each of the four members of the quartet felt deep within that they were climbing a path together that led up to a vertiginous summit. Moving from fortissimo to pianissimo, then back to fortissimo, the two violins perfected their tableau of melancholy solitude, while the viola and cello in unison saw to an energetic bass, always threatening and gradually rising. Finally, when they came to the last chords in A minor, there was a long moment of silence followed by sighs of relief and satisfied smiles.

"Phew!" said Yu. "We stumbled a bit along the way, but it's great we were still able to get through it."

The shadow of a smile crossed his face. Beads of sweat pearled on his brow, furrowed with horizontal lines. He suggested taking a break.

"Gladly," Cheng and Kang said at the same time.

"Shall we have some tea? I'll boil the water," said Yu.

They went to the storage room to put down their instruments.

"I'll take care of it, Mizusawa-san," said Yanfen, her voice clear and lilting.

Once she'd put her instrument in its case, the young woman headed toward the small kitchen across from the storage room, holding the little box of tea that Yu had handed her.

3
.

BY THE TIME YANFEN RETURNED WITH A LARGE WHITE TEAPOT, Yu had placed five dissimilar teacups on a square of navy-blue cloth that covered the two boxes serving as music stands.

"I don't have much sugar. Who would like some?"

"I would," said Rei cheerfully. He had just closed his book.

Yanfen poured the tea into the cups. In the middle of the makeshift table was a plate with some sugar cookies.

"Help yourselves," said Yu unceremoniously.

"But you have to admit, what incredible music!" Kang declared.

"Yes, indeed," Cheng agreed, picking up a sugar cookie and saying, "*Itadakimasu.* I humbly receive."

"The solitude of Schubert the poet, sinking into profound melancholy when he comes up against the violence of an insane world, that is something . . . Like Kang, I will make Mizusawa-san's formula my own; it has gone straight to my heart," said Yanfen.

She continued her thought, adding that the sadness of the melody, voiced above or alongside the dull fear of the bass, was clearly a characteristic of Schubert's composition, something she had encountered fairly frequently in his late piano sonatas.

"Yanfen-san, do you also play the piano?" asked Yu.

"Yes, in China I used to play quite often. But not anymore. I don't have a piano in Tokyo."

"Melancholy is a form of resistance," said Yu. "How is one to remain lucid in a world where reason has been lost, a world that allows itself to be lured by the devil of individual dispossession? Schubert is with us, here and now. He is our contemporary. That is what I feel, deeply."

Rei had already gone back to his bench, after eating two or three cookies dipped in tea. Once again he was absorbed by his book, which he had clearly finished; he was revisiting certain passages, rereading them with renewed attention. But whenever his father spoke, Rei would raise his head to pay ever-increasing attention to what he had to say, although he couldn't fully decipher the meaning of the adult words.

"In any case," said Yu with conviction, "I believe it has meaning, the fact that in our time, in 1938, somewhere in Tokyo, a Sino-Japanese quartet is playing Schubert's *Rosamunde*, while the entire country has succumbed to warmongering obsession; it seems already devoured by the nationalist cancer that divides people into *us* and *them* . . ."

"You're speaking too loudly, Mizusawa-san," murmured Kang.

"Forgive me."

"Who would like some more tea?" asked Yanfen.

Cheng held out his cup.

"And Mizusawa-san?"

"No, thank you. I'm fine."

Yanfen turned to the boy, who was leafing through the pages of his book.

"Would you like some more tea, Rei-kun?"

"Yes, please."

Rei took three long strides to approach Yanfen, and she filled his cup.

"Be careful, it's very hot."

Yanfen, smiling, gave a cookie to Rei, who thanked her shyly, then returned to his bench, cup in hand, taking measured steps so as not to spill the tea.

"I have a question for the three of you," said Yu all of a sudden, "a question that has nothing to do with music."

The three Chinese musicians looked at each other, intrigued by the rather ceremonious tone their Japanese friend had suddenly adopted.

"Why did you decide to stay in Japan when most of the Chinese students who'd come here to study went home last year, after the outbreak of the war now dividing our two countries? It's very brave of you."

Cheng spoke up spontaneously: "It's true that many Chinese have gone home since last year. Our numbers have decreased spectacularly, I think. But some are still coming, in spite of the war. Not many, but a few. The Sino-Japanese Cultural Center is still carrying on its work—"

"You haven't exactly answered Mizusawa-san's question," Yanfen interrupted. "Why are you staying in Tokyo despite undeniable difficulties, certain dangers even, in the present context of war—that was Mizusawa-san's question."

Rei's curiosity was once again aroused by the impeccable construction of the sentence in Japanese, which Yanfen articulated with admirable clarity, as if she were a radio announcer.

He looked up and stared at the adults, who had embarked on a conversation that no longer revolved around Schubert's music.

"I've been living in Tokyo for four years now. Officially I'm still a student, but with the life I lead I'm starting to put down roots. I have friends like you to whom I'm very attached. Then I have a Japanese girlfriend, and I'd like to share my future with her." Cheng turned bright red as if he'd drunk a glassful of beer, something that consistently left him in a state of drowsy intoxication.

"It's true," said Kang in turn, shyly, "our countries have been openly at war since the Marco Polo Bridge incident. But I don't completely identify with China. I'm Chinese, I speak Chinese, but I see myself above all as an individual who's free to choose where he belongs. I try to convince myself that I'm a human being first and foremost, and then Chinese. By the same token, I don't assimilate my Japanese friends with their country. I would like to believe that the bonds of friendship are stronger than national rivalries."

Kang's words, calmly stated in somewhat hesitant Japanese, colored with a particular accent, elicited a reaction from Yanfen. Rei, seated on the bench, his book in his lap, slowly stood up. He went over to Yu and, standing behind him, holding his book tight against his chest all the while, placed his right hand on his father's left shoulder.

"I agree with Kang, and certainly with you, Mizusawa-san. I can say this in all sincerity, since it will remain confidential." Then Yanfen lowered her voice. "Frankly, the Japanese Empire's colonial expansionism fills me with indignation, but that doesn't mean I equate individuals with the state they are said to belong to. In today's world we are, inevitably, subject to the state. And yet we should all identify first and foremost as individuals, above any sense of belonging. To be sure, I'm Chinese and speak Chinese, but I wouldn't like to be reduced to that alone. My individuality, after all, is something entirely different from what was randomly determined by birth."

Absorbed in his friends' thoughts, Yu had forgotten his tea. By the time he emptied his cup, in one go, it was cold. He put the cup down and turned to his three companions, caressing his son's hand, which he felt upon his shoulder. "I am deeply touched by what you're saying. I'd rather have friends like you in an *enemy country* than a despicable homeland with groveling compatriots who swear solely by their affiliation to that homeland. I will be with you and stand by you, even if I end up accused of being 'anti-Japanese,' 'a traitor to the nation,' 'a *hikokumin*.'"

This last word his father had just said, *hikokumin*, made a strong impression on Rei, and he burst out, "Papa, I know that word. I read it in my book. That's the word that Kurokawa's gang uses when they beat up Kitami-kun!"

"That's right, Rei," said Yu, turning to his son. "That's the magic word that powerful people in this country use to crush people who don't obey. They think they're the center of the universe and that *everything revolves around them*, like the influential people Copernicus criticized in his own time. It's an ugly word that dishonors those who say it, not those who are labeled! You will agree: Kitami-kun is right to say no to Kurokawa and all his gang when they order him *to submit because they are older, implying they are right and have greater authority.* Their order is absurd because it's not based on a desire to discern what's fair from what's unfair. Just because someone is older doesn't mean they are right! They don't know how much they degrade themselves by using that terrible word."

As Yu Mizusawa spoke to his son, their Chinese friends listened in silence, astounded.

"Well, maybe it's time to get back to our beloved Schubert," said Yu, glancing at his watch. A luminous smile spread slowly across his face.

It took them only a few minutes to put everything away. Yu put the two cardboard boxes back where they had been. The musicians went and got their instruments from the storage room. When they re-formed their semicircle, Rei also returned and sat in the same place: once again immersed in his book, he hunted for the page where *hikokumin* had been used.

"What shall we do, Mizusawa-san?" asked Kang. "Shall we start on the second movement? Or continue with the first?"

"Uh, what do you think? Shall we attack the Andante?"

"Maybe we could go on to the second movement," said Yanfen, "even if we have to go back later to the Allegro ma non troppo. What do you think, Cheng?"

"Yes, personally I'm eager to see what we come up with, with the Andante. But maybe Mizusawa-san would rather spend a bit more time on the first movement?"

"We still have a long way to go before we're finished with the Allegro ma non troppo, but it's fine with me to begin exploring the second movement."

After a long hesitation, which intrigued the other members of the quartet, Yu continued in a slightly changed tone. With his left hand he was holding the violin upright on his lap, while the bow dangled from his right, almost touching the floor. "This is a total change of subject, but I have a suggestion to make."

Rei, sensitive to the most infinitesimal inflections of his father's voice, trained his gaze on him.

"We are a quartet. We are playing Schubert together. We are all equally small in the presence of this monumental work . . ." The schoolboy closed his book. He didn't move, didn't take his eyes off his father. "But there is a sort of asymmetry which, in my opinion, is regrettable. I mean in the way we are together. All three of you are calling me Mizusawa-san, using my family name, whereas I'm calling you by your first names. Why don't you call me Yu-san?"

"Isn't it difficult or even impossible to call someone by their first name in Japanese?" asked Kang, gently setting his violin and bow on the floor.

"That's true. Normally we don't. Or only under certain conditions, in rare situations that I am at a loss to explain. But this is precisely what I'm doing with you! We could even envisage addressing each other purely and simply by our first names without adding *san*, the way they do in European languages. Would that be too radical?"

"Would you like great freedom and perfect equality to reign, conducive to speaking freely?" said Yanfen to Yu.

"Precisely. So that we can all define ourselves in relation to our shared language. We should be equal before the language and in the language."

A silence fell. It was Yanfen who broke it. She had put her instrument and her bow on her knees, which were pressed together and completely hidden by her dress.

"Since Mizusawa-san—no, Yu-san—no . . . since Yu insists, let's try to create a new space, a new way of being together, through the systematic use of our first names. I think that native speakers can find it difficult to transform their language since they are enclosed within it . . . It is foreigners, rather, who can bring about change!"

"Thank you, Yanfen."

Yu almost said Yanfen-san but managed to stop himself before committing the automatic reflex: the two syllables of the name Yanfen were followed by nothing more than an absence of sound, which produced the striking effect of something being ruthlessly withdrawn.

Rei, who had been following the adults' conversation closely, was stunned by how strange it sounded, his father and the young Chinese woman calling each other by their respective first names.

Yu, inspired by Yanfen's unexpected audacity, continued, "You know, I've been learning French with Philippe, whom you just met. One day he told me something that struck me and made me think. He said that in French they use *the same words* regardless of whom they are speaking to. The words are the same whether you are speaking to a waiter in a restaurant, a taxi driver, a doctor, a professor, or even a cabinet minister."

"Oh my, this is getting complicated," said Cheng, with a twinkle in his eye.

"Yes, I think it's not as easy as it seems. So I've been trying, in my way, to formulate what I think I understood. I think that, for Philippe, language—in his case French—is a commonly held property that users share equitably. Social relations of superiority and inferiority are not embedded the way they are in Japanese."

"I think I'm beginning to understand," said Cheng, keeping his cello squeezed between his legs as if man and instrument were entwined together in a dance.

"When everyone shares a language as if it were common property," said Yanfen, "it is bound to make it easier to achieve horizontal social relations, and to reduce the possibility of one group dominating another."

"Precisely," said Yu, turning to Yanfen. "That's a good thing, isn't it?"

"Particularly in this day and age, I think," she replied, giving Yu a shy smile.

"Imagine a situation where I'm speaking with an important man, my social superior, a minister, for example, precisely . . . If I want to say something about his father, well, I cannot refer to his father in French other than by saying 'your father.' And it's the same for the minister, if he wants to speak about my father."

"He can't name your father in any other way than with 'your father'—like in Chinese, actually," said Cheng.

"Whereas in Japanese," said Kang in turn, "we're obliged to

choose a word that's adapted to our *position* with regard to the person we're speaking to."

"Yes, that's it, that's it exactly," said Yu, approvingly.

"Just as in Japanese we can't use the personal pronoun *you* in a universal way," said Yanfen. "Which is actually a source of frustration to me. I always want to use the equivalent of *you* with whoever is speaking to me. But I know it's not possible."

"Ah, yes," sighed Cheng, with a hint of sadness in his smile, "the impossibility of saying *you* to someone you're speaking to . . ."

After a moment of silence that united all four members of the quartet in a pause for contemplation, Yu suggested they attack the second movement.

Without waiting for the others to react, Yu put his violin under his chin.

Rei, his book closed on his lap, was observing the adults. His attention had not wavered while he followed the conversation between his father and his musician friends.

"Yes, let's go," Kang and Cheng said at the same time.

"The Andante is as melancholy as the Allegro ma non troppo," said Yanfen. "So we'll be continuing our act of resistance . . . won't we, Yu?"

Rei was surprised to hear his father's first name pop up again, and he saw a gracious smile appear on Yanfen's delicately powdered face.

The musicians took up their positions. They were all holding their breath, ready to start. A lasting, absolute silence had fallen among them. Rei, as motionless as a carp at the bottom of a pond in winter, did not take his eyes off them. Finally Yu, hardly breathing, gave the signal to begin with a slight nod of his head.

A simple melody, touching, aching, as transparent as a stream of tears, began to flow from the strings of the first violin.

The schoolboy, as if transfixed with astonishment or admiration, made himself pure hearing, and he could feel something rising inside him, gradually, right up to the back of his ears—a shiver of emotion, mingled with a rush of warmth. The four instrumentalists, occasionally exchanging a knowing glance, smiled like children sculpted by Carpeaux. The first violin continued its delicate tracing of the melodic line, with a sweetness that came from deep within, while the three other instruments supported it, like a solid pedestal carrying a great goddess made of fragile ceramic.

Suddenly Schubert's music was harshly dispelled by the unintelligible clamor of men and the pounding of boots rushing in, violently and en masse, headed for the floor above.

Instinctively, Yu sprang up and ran to his son, his violin and bow in his left hand. He grabbed his son's left arm and told him to hide at once in the big wardrobe. Rei rushed to it.

"Don't move until I come back! All right?"

"Ah, Coper!" shouted Rei.

Yu turned around, grabbed the book, which was still on the bench, and gave it to his son, who was already in the wardrobe;

then the boy immediately closed the door. Yu rushed into the storage room, placed his violin and bow into their case, and came back out at once. He leaned against the wall, breathing heavily.

The three Chinese musicians, flabbergasted, glanced at him without a word. He looked back and smiled.

4.

IN THE PENUMBRA, REI WONDERED WHAT WAS HAPPENING, what would happen. Why did he have to stay there, alone, in that dark hiding place? For how long? No matter how many times he asked himself, no answer came.

Before long, he could hear a commotion. So as not to make a disturbance, he took off his shoes and placed them beneath his bent knees. The keyhole shone like a star in a dark sky. He slowly put his right eye to it. He stopped short an inch from the star. It projected a luminous ray onto his iris, appearing like a planet orbiting it.

His eyelids blinked, twice.

5

·

AT THE PRECISE INSTANT YU, HAVING LEFT HIS VIOLIN IN THE storage room, returned to his quartet, the door to the large meeting room was thrown open. Five soldiers in khaki and matching field caps barged in noisily. The smallest, a squat, hairy man with a haughty manner, immediately began to probe his surroundings, hands clenched behind his back, while the remaining soldiers stood erect opposite Yu, rifles in hand. Yu, in the meantime, had joined his three Chinese friends, who clutched their instruments tightly. The hairy soldier opened the storage room door but presently shut it after a brief survey of its scattered contents. He passed the bench, headed toward the massive wardrobe, and stared at it for a while as if he had never before seen the likes of it. The boy inside dared not glance through the keyhole. As he trembled with fear, it seemed that he could hear the rustle of the soldier's uniform through the door, and even his breathing as he exhaled noisily, brazenly, like a man in a furious rage. The soldier returned unhurriedly to the musicians, who were being watched by his subordinates. Looking Yu up and down, he broke the silence.

"What are you doing here?" he demanded, impertinently.

"We're musicians," Yu immediately replied. "We were rehearsing."

"With the black curtains closed?"

"It makes it easier to concentrate. It's quieter, too."

"And what sort of music were you rehearsing?"

"Franz Schubert's String Quartet in A Minor, opus 29. It's more commonly known as *Rosamunde*."

"That's not something of ours, is it?"

The soldier moved to face Yanfen. "And you, were you doing the same thing?" He looked her straight in the eyes.

Rei couldn't decipher what was said after that. He recognized his father's voice but had trouble hearing him. Then his voice was cut off. After five or six excruciating seconds, he heard his father's warm cadence resume, but now unusually tense.

"Yes, this is my wife . . . Aiko. She plays the viola."

For a split second, Yanfen shot Yu a fleeting look.

"Yes, with my husband, who is first violin," she said, with overriding confidence. "We've been rehearsing Schubert's quartet for several weeks."

"Well, say, you have a really young wife!" mocked the squat man.

Mindless, sarcastic mirth surfaced upon the four soldiers' faces, which had, until then, remained silent and impassive.

"And the other two, these gentlemen?" continued the officer with disdain.

"They are both," Yu explained hurriedly, stammering, "they are . . . they are both scholarship students from the Sino-Japanese Study Center. They're our friends. They play music with us to relax."

"You socialize with Chinks! You play the music of *hairy*

white people, suspicious foreigners! Enemy countries! You're piling them on, your serious crimes!"

"Sir, please be polite to our friends and guests. Take back that slur you just used! And besides, Schubert is Austrian. Austria has, unfortunately, been annexed by Nazi Germany. So, Schubert's music is not enemy music after all, if you'll allow me to point that out . . . sir."

The hairy soldier went up to Yu. He was bright red. Now only four inches away from Yu, his face was flushed with subdued fury.

"We are at war with the Chinks. Is this any time to go casually fiddling with your *guests*?"

The soldier pronounced *guests* with all the hate he could muster.

"The great Polish conductor Joseph Rosenstock settled in Japan last year to lead the New Symphony Orchestra. We play European music in Japan, sir. Music crosses borders; it belongs to all humanity."

"You wouldn't happen to be a Red, by any chance? Only communists talk like you!"

A mad, destructive rage overcame the man in uniform, his entire body beginning to shudder.

Rei's father's words reached him in the gloom of the wardrobe, echoing faintly like the words of farewell a traveler tries to convey to his beloved through the train's glass as it pulls away. Rei didn't want to miss anything his father said, but his attention was greatly distressed by that wild, fulminating voice that sowed terror throughout the hall. "No, sir, I am not a communist. I am simply telling you what my reason dictates."

"So it's your reason that dictates? Ha! An intellectual stuffed with diplomas!"

Incensed, the squat man spat straight in his face. Yu wiped his eyes and cheeks with the sleeve of his jacket.

"Are the four of you really here to play music? Not for some other reason? This music isn't some sort of pretext? You don't have an instrument, so far as I can tell."

"Sir, if you would like, I can show you my violin. I left it in the storage room. Do I have your permission to go and retrieve it?"

Without waiting for the enraged soldier's permission, Yu moved toward the storage room.

Rei heard footsteps. No one spoke.

The moment Yu opened the storage room door the soldiers, already facing him, immediately prepared to charge. Yu vanished, then reappeared in the doorway with his violin. He walked back to the soldier.

"Here is my violin, sir."

Yu handed his instrument to the furious man, who took it in his hands and examined it as if he were discovering, handling, a stringed instrument for the first time.

"What's your name, Mr. Friend-of-Chinks?" The officer's eyes glowed red with hate.

"Mizusawa."

Rei thought he could hear his father utter his surname. He wanted to see what was happening. Once again the little planet orbited the star.

"You fail to show respect, Mizusawa! Respect with regard to the soldiers of His Majesty the Emperor!"

On saying "His Majesty the Emperor," the squat man stood
to attention for two or three seconds as if he really were in the
sovereign's presence.

"You deserve to be taught a lesson!"

Before he had finished saying "lesson," he clipped Yu hard
in the face. Yu fell. But he got back up. And the officer immediately struck him again, harder than before. Yu collapsed again.
Yanfen instinctively bent down, clinging to him, her viola and
bow on the floor. She took Yu's arm and turned to glare at his
assailant, her gaze gleaming with anger.

"It is my job to reform *hikokumins* like you!" he roared.

Possessed by his fervent hate, he slammed the instrument
to the floor with all his strength before stamping on it with
his hefty leather boots. The violin—splintered, flattened,
pulverized—let out eerie cries of agony, beyond any a dying
animal might make in a ruthless hunter's forest.

Rei witnessed the entire intolerable scene through the keyhole, unable to grasp all the words exchanged between his
father and the officer. He was horribly shaken by the violence
his father was subjected to. Paralyzed with fear, curled in a
ball, crippled by a child's helplessness, all he could do in the
darkness of his hiding was fret. The only thing he heard now,
reverberating deep within his ear canal, was the hideousness
of the word *hikokumin* and the evanescent cries, plaintive and
dissonant, of his father's dying violin.

6
.

SOMEONE HAD JUST ARRIVED. REI, HOLDING HIS BOOK IN HIS hands, listened. A confused jumble of footsteps and words. Amid the muddle of sound, the savage officer's voice suddenly rang out: "Lieutenant, sir!"

7.

A TALL, SLENDER OFFICER, HIS MANNER CALM AND SOLEMN, A
saber at his side, entered the room alongside several soldiers.
The squat, hairy soldier and his four fellows immediately
turned to him and bowed.

"At ease! There's no one upstairs, nothing suspicious. What
is happening here, Corporal Tanaka?"

So that was the terrible soldier's name, thought Rei in the
gloom of his hiding place. Tanaka maintained his posture,
heels together, arms to his side, and he replied, "Lieutenant,
sir, I was questioning these suspicious individuals about their
activities with the black curtains pulled shut. They claim to be
practicing music together, but personally, I'm tempted to think
they were holding a secret meeting disguised as a musical
rehearsal."

A questioning look on his face, the lieutenant listened to his
deputy's account and peered at the broken violin on the floor.
His gaze also took in the four people assembled, immured in
silence, clearly wary, as defensive as they were frightened. The
lieutenant noticed that the young woman supported the arm
of a man with a swollen face and disheveled hair, blood oozing
from his mouth. The lieutenant interrupted Tanaka, pointing
with his chin at the broken instrument.

"Why is this violin smashed?"

"I did it, sir."

"Why?"

"Because that man," answered the corporal, pointing at Yu, "said disrespectful things about the soldiers of His Majesty the Emperor."

As he had done a few minutes earlier, Tanaka immediately stood at attention to underscore *His Majesty the Emperor*.

"Have you no idea, Corporal Tanaka, how much a violin can cost, how much human effort it can represent?" said the lieutenant, his voice calm, a touch disillusioned.

"I wanted, sir, to reprimand a thug, a *hikokumin*, a communist who plays music with Chinks while we are at war."

Rei, cringing and sequestered in the dark cavern of the wardrobe, was horrified to hear the word uttered again in the coarse soldier's booming voice.

The lieutenant turned to the injured man and asked politely for the name of the piece they had been rehearsing.

"Schubert's String Quartet in A Minor, opus 29, D. 804, sir."

"*Rosamunde.*"

"Yes, that's it. Do you know it?"

"Yes, a little. It's a magnificent piece."

"Absolutely. We've been practicing it for several weeks. My wife, Aiko, and our two Chinese friends, Mr. Kang Song and Mr. Cheng Wang."

The lieutenant bowed slightly, giving them a military salute. The two men and Yanfen, her arm still tucked in Yu's, nodded discreetly.

"So this is your violin?" asked the lieutenant, both troubled and embarrassed.

"Yes. It's in a sorrowful state, poor thing."

Through the broken soundboard, the lieutenant could see the soul post, broken in two.

"Is it an old violin from a master luthier?"

"It's not a Stradivarius, of course," Yu replied, laughing with faint irony, slightly embarrassed, "but it is an old instrument, made by a French luthier whose name was Nicolas François Vuillaume. It dates from 1857. I don't think it's very valuable. It didn't cost very much, or at least much less than any of the violins made by his older brother, Jean-Baptiste."

"And you play first violin, mister . . . ?"

"My name is Mizusawa. Yes, I'm the first violin."

On hearing his family name in his father's baritone, Rei shivered in the wardrobe's deadened gloom.

"Mr. Mizusawa, would you play something for us, to show us that you really were practicing music? It would be ideal if you could grant us the pleasure of performing *Rosamunde* with your wife and friends, but unfortunately your violin is in this pitiful state, due to a regrettable misunderstanding."

The lieutenant thought he could hear the faint rustle of uniforms behind him, the imperceptible exhalation of suppressed breath, while Corporal Tanaka, after twice rubbing his throat, presented a face twitching from nervous tension, its skin tingling.

"I can try to play a piece by Bach, if Mr. Song will kindly lend me his violin."

"Would you agree to lend him your instrument, Mr. Song?" the lieutenant asked courteously.

"It would be my pleasure. No doubt it will not do justice

to your talent, Mr. Mizusawa; but I could only feel immensely honored if you would play Bach on my violin."

Kang handed Yu his instrument.

"Thank you, Kang. I'll go and get my bow, if you don't mind."

"Please, Mr. Mizusawa."

Yu pulled away from Yanfen's arm, tenderly squeezing her shoulder. Then he went to the storage room, coming back with his bow. He tuned the violin, infinitesimally adjusting the four pegs with the fingers of his left hand, while the bow in his right tapped the four strings one after the other; now and again he also turned the tuner. Finally, after a long minute, he was ready. He closed his eyes and took a deep breath. Then he opened his eyes.

"I shall begin."

Yu gave his musician friends a sweet, affectionate smile, and saluted the lieutenant with a slight nod.

He placed the bow on the strings. A meditative song, calm, serene, profound, transparently clear, rose gradually into the almost religious silence that nothing could disturb and no one dared interrupt.

8

.

LEANING FORWARD, UPRIGHT, SWAYING FROM SIDE TO SIDE, YU played with his eyes closed. The piece began with a buoyant theme—jovial, bright, an adolescent's accompaniment from town as he sets out one sunny morning to walk through the countryside, driven by his happiness to be alive, stirred by his eagerness to explore the beauty of the surrounding landscape. At a certain point the music turned somber, as if conveying his apprehension on suddenly seeing a black mass of cloud on the horizon, which had been clear and radiant only minutes earlier. But it was only a fleeting darkness. Not long thereafter the cheer of the initial theme resurfaced. How many times had they already heard it, this smiling, sparkling motif? What was obvious, in its insistent reoccurrence, in this desire to end-lessly *embroider* it, was the composer's unwavering devotion to its jolly little melody, like the unconditional affection felt for a simple childhood tune that still resonates deeply, unin-terrupted, like an inexhaustible spring, ready to gush forth at any second, from early youth to advanced age. But the stroll had to come to an end. The music suddenly faltered. The vio-linist's body, moving right to left, left to right, suddenly eased forward, as if concentrating all its energy on punctuating the final resurgence of the theme, fashioned until then in several subtle iterations. The piece had lasted barely three minutes.

Three minutes during which the notes had fallen one by one like silver raindrops on bamboo after a fierce downpour. When the bow was lifted, the last note was followed by silence.

Yu opened his eyes and looked at his friends. A timid applause could be heard, quickly repressed. The lieutenant, who had listened from beginning to end, eyes closed, head down, hands clasped behind his hips, now looked up at the violinist.

"Partita no. 3 in E Major by Johann Sebastian Bach, the Gavotte en rondeau," said the lieutenant, his voice trembling.

"If I had known, I would have prepared. Just now I rather feel I ruined this masterpiece—"

"No, Mr. Mizusawa, you played magnificently."

Yu thought he could detect in the officer's eyes, where he stood just below the pale neon light, the discreet trace of a tear.

"Are you a professional musician?" asked the lieutenant.

"No, I'm an English teacher. I play as an amateur. I love music. I consider music—even when it comes from elsewhere, a country with whom we are at war—to be the heritage of all humanity . . ."

"*Rosamunde* and the Gavotte will outlive us, that much is certain. In any case, thank you very much, Mr. Mizusawa, for playing for us. I believe it is now obvious that Mr. Mizusawa and his friends were playing music here. We may clear them of suspicion, don't you think, Corporal Tanaka?"

The soldier did not reply and continued to stand as he had since the lieutenant arrived, straight as a candle, staring into the void, trembling with stifled irritation.

9.

IT WAS THEN THAT A SOLDIER RUSHED INTO THE ROOM AND addressed the lieutenant.

"I am here to inform you of an order from headquarters, sir."

"Yes, and what is it?"

"All interrogated suspects must be taken to headquarters without exception, sir."

"All interrogated persons?"

"Yes, sir."

"Without exception?"

"Yes, sir."

Corporal Tanaka's face loosened for a fraction of a second. The squat soldier, whom his superior ignored, was rejoicing inside, without causing the slightest outward disturbance. And yet everyone could hear, plainly, the silent fanfare of his sardonic snickering.

"You have heard, Mr. Mizusawa," said the lieutenant in a hushed voice, going closer to Yu. "I am obliged to see that you are taken to headquarters. Your wife and friends, too. I hope you will be released promptly. Corporal!" he shouted.

"Yes, sir."

Tanaka, standing straighter, directed his gaze at his superior's cap.

"Your orders are to take them to headquarters. Proceed."

"Yes—"

Before the corporal could finish his reply, Yanfen coldly interrupted by picking up her instrument, which had been placed on the floor during Yu's assault.

"Please, sir, give us the time to put away our instruments."

"Naturally, madam. Please, go ahead."

Yanfen and the other two musicians went to the storage room without a word and cased their instruments. As soon as they came out, Corporal Tanaka ordered his men to escort "the suspicious couple and the Chinks." In the span of a few seconds the room was emptied. The lieutenant alone remained, enveloped in a sudden silence disturbed only by the receding footsteps.

10

HIS GAZE FELL ONTO THE MUTILATED VIOLIN. HE CROUCHED down. He took it gingerly into his hands—this suffering body, its four strings loosely forming tormented curves like the tubing and electric wires that cover the face of a gravely injured accident victim or the survivor of an indiscriminate bombing. He wondered what to do with it. Noticing the European wardrobe at the back of the room, next to a bench with a backrest, he wondered how its silent mass had ended up here, in an obscure municipal cultural center. Approaching, he paused before it, the height of the wardrobe noticeably less than its slender width. With necessary care, he placed the violin on the bench to the left of the wardrobe, as if gently laying a baby to sleep in a Moses basket. Then he delicately opened— as if excusing himself for the indiscretion—the door to the wardrobe, its upper edge hardly reaching any higher than his chest. Light filtered in, partitioning the interior into haphazard zones of shadow and light by introducing an oblique dividing line. A child's feet, clothed in green socks, entered his field of vision. He was struck dumb by the abrupt appearance of white skin on little legs, bare to the knees. Then the child's hand, shaking, reached timidly for a book just next to his feet. The lieutenant had just the time to catch the title: *How Do You Live?* He began to bend, slowly, very slowly, as if hesitating . . . His eyes, shining like those of a cat lurking in the half-light, met the boy's, pale with fear. He smiled, not wanting to frighten him. Then he reached toward the bench next to them, on his left, and picked up the violin. Suddenly, a man's voice shouted in the distance, like the sound of a trumpet rehearsing backstage: "Kurokami! Kurokami!"

Mechanically, the lieutenant cocked his head, as if wondering where exactly the voice was coming from and trying to identify its owner. His face contracted tensely. Not saying a word, he handed the boy the broken violin, almost flattened, its four strings forming a rounded contour that in the darkness resembled a small injured animal. The child hesitated, but in the end, fainthearted, he took the damaged instrument into both hands.

"Kurokami! Lieutenant Kurokami!"

The lieutenant thought he recognized Captain Honjo's voice.

He hurried to close the door, staring all the while, one final glance, at the trembling boy. The worried, distraught look he flashed was followed by the ghost of a smile—quickly erased upon the captain's approach.

"Oh, there you are! What on earth are you doing here, Kurokami? We're leaving. No time to mess around."

"Yes, sir! Forgive me, I was just making sure we hadn't overlooked anything."

In the darkness of the wardrobe, Rei distinctly heard the hard male voice he thought belonged to the man who had shouted, "Kurokami!" only seconds earlier. He was surprised to hear the name Kurokami, because he had never dreamed a last name could mean "black hair." The man was saying something the child couldn't grasp very well; his tone was commanding or like that of someone who was very angry. He frightened Rei. Another male voice replied quite calmly, evenly, almost gently. Was that the voice of the man who had given him the violin?

Gradually the voices receded. The footsteps, too. Rei remained in darkness. Before long he couldn't hear anything. Or rather, at the periphery of his ears he heard something like the faint, stubborn trill of dying cicadas. It was tinnitus, a word he had learned from his father not long ago. It was the sound of silence . . . He peered through the keyhole. The room was dark because the black curtains had been drawn, but there was enough light from the neons to convince him no one was there anymore. What time was it? Night had not yet fallen, but he was starting to get hungry. He listened . . . and convinced himself that really, there was no one there anymore, not a soul in sight. So, he lifted the latch as quietly as possible, trying not to make the slightest noise as he opened the door. But it creaked. "Shut up!" he thought. He waited a little. Nothing new; it was still as silent. There was no one there anymore. He put his canvas shoes back on—he'd taken them off, to not make any noise. He left his hiding place, the broken violin in his hands, and his book in the pocket of his trousers. He took a few timid steps; he was having trouble walking: Ah! His legs had gone to sleep! He stopped. He waited a few seconds. He started walking again. He crossed the big hall and went toward the door. With all his weight he pushed the heavy entrance door. Now he was standing outside the municipal cultural center. He looked up at the sky. Day was departing. The veil of night was beginning to cover the cloud-spotted sky. Without his father, he felt helpless and alone. Sobs caught in his throat. A huge black force was crushing him, projecting shapeless suffocating shadows onto him. People walked by in the street. Soldiers from the military police, with rifles on their shoulders, were on patrol. Rei couldn't see a single child around. Where had his papa gone? Would he be coming back? Or would he go straight home? Rei started down the street that led home. He hurried his steps . . . cradling the ruined violin, as if it were a dying animal he had to protect against a predator, against the fiendish cruelty of a ruthless hunter.

11

.

THE MORE THE NIGHT REPLACED DAY, THE RARER THE PRESENCE
of figures. Rei had been walking for more than ten minutes
to reach his house, located roughly twenty minutes from
the cultural center. He had taken several narrow streets that
wound their way like a labyrinth, but as he had gone this way
a number of times with his father, he had no difficulty finding
his way home.

When he reached a small intersection, the street lamp's
bare bulb weakly illuminating a patch of bamboo hedge that
hid a cherry sapling's trunk, he noticed the presence of a Shiba
Inu. With neither collar nor leash, it stood motionless behind
the tall lamppost, its triangular ears erect, and stared at the
schoolboy, wagging left to right a tail that curled naturally over
its back. Rei slowed his steps. He was afraid the dog would
be startled by a human approaching in the dark and might
leap at him and bite. So Rei was careful not to meet its gaze.
He walked by very slowly, ignoring the creature's silent attention. He went on for twenty yards or so before, still walking, he
turned around fearfully to see whether he'd managed to avoid
being pursued. But he hadn't—the dog was still there, trailing
him, only five or six yards away. The child quickened his pace,
then stopped short. And the dog stopped, too. It did not take
its eyes off him. Rei realized the Shiba's curled tail still moved

like a pendulum. He started walking again, went on a dozen or so yards, then turned. The same. The dog had followed him and still trailed him at the same distance from which he had stopped and observed him a few moments earlier. Rei understood that the dog did not wish to harm him. Now he was very near his house. He crouched down, watching the dog; a lantern a few yards away tinted its coat bronze. Then the dog slowly approached. Their heads, both about twenty inches from the ground, almost touched, as if they were about to kiss. They looked at each other in silence. Finally, Rei dared hold out his hand. After a moment's hesitation, the dog extended its paw.

"Are you all alone, too?"

Rei kept the Shiba's white paw in his hand for a long time. Their two shadows, mingled, overlapping, were cast onto the uneven surface of the narrow dirt road.

"Do you want to come with me?"

Rei stood up and set off again, looking down at the dog. It walked alongside him, next to his left leg, raising its placid eyes toward the schoolboy's face.

"You're coming with me! You're not going home? Are you alone, too?"

The child stopped, bent down, and took the dog's neck between his hands. Far from protesting, the dog put up no resistance. Their eyes met. The dog remained still, and the boy thought he could see something like a dancing flame in its dilated pupils. Suddenly the dog licked Rei's face, making inarticulate little whimpers.

"Okay. Let's go," said Rei.

A few minutes later they arrived at a double sliding wooden door. It was the entrance to Yu Mizusawa's house, as indicated on a little wooden plaque placed above, where the three ideograms corresponding to his first and last name were meticulously calligraphed. The house, which Yu Mizusawa rented, was black and painted, made of planks and bordered by an identical house. Both were pitch dark, feebly lit by the ghostly orange glow of a flimsy wooden street lamp.

"This is my house. *Otōsan*, Father, isn't home yet. I can't get in; he's the one with the key. We'll wait for him here."

The Shiba gazed at Rei while the boy spoke, trying to convince himself of his father's imminent return. Autumn was progressively settling in, ever deeper, the thermometer dropping to a temperature that brought a chill as soon as night fell. Rei was beginning to feel cold. The shorts he wore—on Sundays, like many of his friends, he always wore shorts, until the beginning of winter—didn't make matters better. He nestled against the double sliding door. The dog had been sitting on its hindquarters, but the instant the boy curled up, trying to keep out the cold, it slid gently between the boy's chest and his legs, which were tucked beneath him. Rei felt the dog's warm belly; moments later it closed its eyes. Before long he, too, drifted off.

12
.

"REI-KUN, WHAT ARE YOU DOING THERE?"

The boy was woken by a man's voice. He raised his head, rubbing his eyes.

"Ah, Filippu-san . . ."

"What are you doing here alone at such an hour?"

The Shiba, pressed tightly against Rei's little body, abruptly swiveled its head to stare questioningly at the evening caller's stunned face.

II

ANDANTE

1

.

THE PHONE RANG.

"Hello?"

"Jacques, it's me. Are you listening to France Musique?"

"No, I'm in the middle of something rather tricky. What's going on?"

The old man, his hair white and receding, peered into the void above his progressive lenses, the frame slipping down his nose.

"They've just announced that a twenty-three-year-old Japanese woman won first prize at the Ludwig van Beethoven International Violin Competition in Berlin. It was yesterday. Her name is Midori Yamazaki."

Jacques did not respond.

"Hello? Are you listening?"

Still no response.

"Hello, Jacques, are you listening?"

"Yes, forgive me. Yes, of course, I'm listening."

"So, have you ever heard of Midori Yamazaki?"

"No . . . I don't think so. Uh, well, maybe . . . Hang on . . . yes, someone mentioned a certain Midori recently . . . Could it have been Midori Yamazaki? I'm not sure . . ."

"You know, I found it easy to remember her name because it's like the whisky . . ."

"Oh, right. You know, Yamazaki is a very common last name in Japan. Midori, too, for that matter—you hear that first name a lot. Well, there's Midori Goto, for example . . . There must be dozens of Yamazakis and hundreds of Midoris in the music world . . ."

"Since you know quite a few Japanese musicians, I wanted to see whether the name meant anything to you, that's all."

"Maybe someone told me about her, but I don't automatically pay attention to every Japanese name. You know, it's not all that rare nowadays for a Japanese man or woman to win a prize in an international competition . . ."

"Yes, you're right. Well, I won't be late. See you—"

"How are you, Hélène? Did it go okay today?"

"Yes, I'm fine. I'll tell you about my meeting with the cellist! And on your end?"

"No problem. I'm waiting for the violinist. Anyway, see you tonight!"

"Yes. I'll go shopping on my way home. Do you want me to grab anything?"

"No, nothing in particular."

The old man put down the phone. He was wearing a navy-blue apron spotted here and there with minute wood shavings. He returned to his long, narrow workbench where, beside a cello with its soundboard removed for restoration, lay a violin or viola in the process of being made, its wood still unvarnished and bare. The instrument did not yet have a neck or fingerboard, but its hourglass body was complete, its constituent parts carefully assembled and meticulously put together. The man in the navy-blue apron inspected his object with an air of satisfaction, holding it in his left hand. The f-holes reminded him, as they often did, of the long slanted eyes of a Japanese Okame mask. They transfigured the surface of the gracefully rounded soundboard into the face of a smiling, radiant woman. On the opposite wall hung an incredible variety of carpenters' and luthiers' tools. Higher up, a framed diploma was visible, from the Cremona Scuola Internazionale di Liuteria. After a few minutes had passed, his eyes left his child, still in a fetal state, to address the numerous stringed instruments hanging vertically from the wooden board, painted entirely white, a dozen or so yards in length, that ran horizontally just below the ceiling from one end of the wall to the other. He turned his chair toward his collection of perfectly arranged violins and violas. A medium-size short-haired dog, dozing at its master's feet, now suddenly raised its head and gazed for a long while at the old man.

"No, not yet, Momo. It's only four o'clock. A little later, all right?"

For a split second the dog's triangle ears perked up on its head of light brown fur and twitched to catch the old man's words.

The man in the navy-blue apron removed his glasses, held by a chain. He slowly massaged his eyelids with the fingers of both hands, the way watchmakers and artisans in other professions do, tired after a long day's work, the sort that demands extreme concentration. He opened his eyes. His gaze was lost in the void. He became pensive, then eventually closed his eyes again. Leaning back against the chair, arms crossed, he lapsed into a state of silent contemplation, emerging from it only several prolonged minutes later.

He rose to his feet and headed toward the kitchen through the little sitting area where three black leather armchairs encircled a low rectangular glass table. Having made some coffee, he sat in the armchair nearest the built-in bookshelf at the end of the room. Then, the bitch—because Momo is a female dog's name—came in turn to lie at his feet.

The man in the navy-blue apron lifted his eyes once more to the instruments fastened to the horizontal plank.

He finished his coffee, got up, and before returning to work, turned on the radio, where a woman's voice—smooth, flowing, pleasing—was saying, "You have been listening to the String Quartet no. 3 in D Major, opus 18, by Ludwig van Beethoven, performed by the Alban Berg Quartet."

Someone rang the doorbell.

2
.

THE LUTHIER OPENED THE DOOR. A MAN IN HIS THIRTIES WAS standing there.

"Good afternoon. Christophe Rubens, I'm a bit early. I hope that's not a problem?"

"No, not at all. Very nice to meet you. Jacques Maillard."

"Pleased to meet you. David Tréchard sent me."

"Yes, I know. Come in."

The old man led the young man into the little sitting area.

"Thank you for agreeing to see me on such short notice."

"You're welcome. You have a concert tomorrow evening, I believe?"

"Precisely. But my violin has not been right ever since I got back to Paris the day before yesterday. It doesn't sound the way it usually does."

"Did you travel by plane? Where were you before?"

"Saint Petersburg."

"And before Saint Petersburg?"

"Mumbai, in India."

"And before Mumbai?"

"Canada."

"Your violin has almost certainly suffered from so much traveling. Let me have a look."

The two men, in the little sitting area, were still standing.

"Have a seat," said the luthier. "Would you like coffee? I also have tea."

"Um . . . tea would be nice—that's kind of you."

"What sort of tea? Black or green? I have both."

"Green, please."

Jacques disappeared into the kitchen. Christophe Rubens looked around: he was impressed by the considerable number of violins and violas that hung from the wall. He had never seen this many in a luthier's workshop. Against the wall, opposite the violins and violas, stood three cellos; one impressed him with its extremely dark hue, reminding him of a masterpiece by Domenico Montagnana he'd admired years earlier in a Hungarian musician's home in Budapest.

Jacques returned. Two cups were set on a round red tray: one, porcelain, without a handle, decorated with little motifs of blue flowers, the other black ceramic with a rustic appearance. The luthier set the tray down on the glass table. He sat across from the violinist and offered him the porcelain teacup. A silence fell. The two men took their first swallow of tea.

"Your tea is excellent."

"You think so? You like it? It's not too strong?"

"No, no, it's just the way I like it."

Jacques finished his tea.

"Right, let me have a look at your violin."

The violinist handed the luthier his instrument, which he'd been holding on his lap.

"Thank you. I hope that a quick tune-up will be enough. Well, then, I won't be long." Jacques took the violin and went to his workbench. He put on his glasses, lit the desk lamp, opened the case, and took out the violin to immediately begin examining it.

"But it's a Vuillaume, your violin!" cried the luthier from his workbench, finding it hard to hide his enthusiasm.

"Yes, didn't David tell you?" replied Christophe loudly, not moving from the armchair.

A deep silence settled over the room. All that could be heard, from time to time, was the almost imperceptible sound of some delicate, painstaking operation, with gestures hard to imagine. Roughly half an hour passed, and all the while Christophe had nothing more to do than gaze at the instruments on display, the books on instrument making, and the considerable array of CDs that filled the bookshelf.

Finally, the luthier appeared with the violin and bow in hand.

"Please, try it."

He placed the violin and its bow on the solid wooden table that separated the little sitting area from the actual workshop. The violinist sprang to his feet. He began tuning the violin, making short bow strokes on the strings.

"I can see it's better already."

"It needed adjusting . . . dare I say, some *care* . . . I replaced the bridge. It wasn't straight and the strings had dug in a bit too deep. I think it hadn't been changed in quite a while. Then I moved the sound post a tenth of a millimeter . . . I think it really suffered from its recent bout of being battered around the planet—as I said. A violin is a sensitive creature, you know . . ."

Then, without responding to the luthier's remark, Christophe Rubens launched into the Bach Chaconne. Jacques sank deep into his armchair to listen to the piece he had heard countless times. During his long years of training, how often had his craftsmanship been sorely tested by this compositional showpiece for violin! Every time, it provided him with an opportunity to try and prove himself equal to the world of sound now emanating from an instrument he knew like the back of his hand.

Once the violinist had finished playing the beginning of the Chaconne, with its passages of double, triple, and even quadruple stopping, he paused.

"This is perfect, Monsieur Maillard. I'm glad to have my violin back, just the way I remember it."

"That's good to hear. That's a fine instrument you have there! A Vuillaume is not to be scoffed at."

"Yes, and I'm very happy with it. And you've been its savior . . . and mine, of course. I am sincerely grateful. How much do I owe you?"

"Well . . . a hundred and fifty euros—does that sound fair?"

"That is fine. May I write you a check?"

"Of course."

Christophe Rubens took out his checkbook, and while signing, he turned for a second to the violins and violas hanging on the wall.

"Are they your work?" he asked.

"Yes, most of them. There are four I didn't make. But the rest are mine. There are thirty-eight of them in total."

"May I try a few?"

"Yes, if you'd like."

Jacques Maillard went over to his parade of instruments. Examining them closely, he chose three and set them down on the big table. "These are three instruments I made at various stages of my career. I'm very attached to all three of them. You can try them. You'll let me know what you think."

Christophe Rubens again played the Bach Chaconne on the three violins Jacques Maillard had suggested. He spent two or three minutes on each, and found them all very fine, by virtue of the crystal-clear, slightly bluish limpidity of the high notes as well as the nocturnal, telluric depth of the basses. He was also struck by a rare, remarkable evenness to the sound.

"I like all three of them. But I know which one I would choose. I don't dare ask you the price . . ."

"The third one is not for sale. But the other two . . . I'm open to discussion. Come back and see me if you would like to buy either of them. And there are others, as you can see. Some of them more affordable . . ."

"What a pity! A real pity! Indeed, I would have chosen the third one . . ."

"Oh, really?"

"It's different from the other two . . . I think it's extraordinary, the clarity and fullness of its sound are absolutely captivating."

"You think so? Indeed, it's not like the others. You can tell . . . you've sensed the difference . . ."

"Monsieur Maillard, I will be back. I can't say when, but I will be back, that much is for certain. I'd like to become better acquainted with your work. I'll leave you my contact details."

The violinist took out a business card and handed it to the luthier, who reciprocated.

"You have all my information here: address, phone number, email, and the hours for the workshop."

"Right. Thank you very much."

The old man in the navy-blue apron saw the musician out. Then he closed the glass door and flipped the little sign so that visitors would see the word *Closed*.

He went back to what he'd been working on.

3
.

JACQUES AND HÉLÈNE HAD FINISHED FILLING THE DISHWASHER.
Momo, her bowl emptied long before her human companions
had finished dinner, had already curled up in her usual spot
next to the L-shaped sofa in the large living room. This living
room was divided from Jacques's workshop by a thick partitioning wall that opened, on the workshop side, onto the little
sitting area. Momo was waiting for her master, the way she did
every evening after dinner.

"I have to show you what I found in *Libé*."

Hélène took the newspaper from her little backpack, which
she had left on the sofa when she arrived. With her index finger
she pointed out a paragraph in the cultural spread on the oval
coffee table.

"I found this after I called this afternoon. A feature on Midori
Yamazaki, first prize at the Ludwig van Beethoven International
Violin Competition."

Hélène stood staring at Jacques while he bent down to rub
his Shiba's head.

"You'll see, it's very interesting, what they wrote. Shall I
make some tea, as usual?"

"Yes, that would be nice."

Hélène came back a few minutes later with a teapot and
two handleless cups on the round red lacquered tray Jacques

had used to serve Christophe Rubens. She'd also placed two madeleines on a little plate. She settled on the sofa next to Jacques.

"Look, she's had a brilliant career so far."

Picking up the newspaper, Hélène began reading out loud a few of the lines devoted to the young Japanese violinist: "'A graduate of the Tokyo National University of Fine Arts and Music, she continued her musical education in New York, Geneva, and Paris, studying with great masters of the violin such as David Zukerman, Michel Steinberg, and Jean-Jacques Aulard. She was born into a family of amateur musicians. But by her own admission it was her maternal grandfather who played a vital role in her musical awakening, as well as her choice of a career in music. She plays a Stradivarius, on loan from the Japan Foundation.'"

Once Hélène had finished reading, she reached for her teacup, taking a swallow of roasted green tea, which she drank in the evening to ensure a good night's sleep.

"There must be dozens of Japanese musicians who come to Europe every year to perfect their technique," said Jacques.

"There are indeed a lot of them. I even have a few among my clientele!"

"Some of them manage to make a name for themselves, positioning themselves among their fellow European artists, and they're on their way to an international career. That's certainly the case for this Midori Yamazaki. But there are some who disappear, as well . . ."

"We'll be following her, that's for sure . . ."

Jacques didn't answer. He finished his tea in one swallow.

"So your cellist came back to see you?"

"Yes. She finally chose one. It took her long enough. She kept hesitating, and hesitating, and hesitating . . . But now I think she'll be one of my loyal clients. In any case, she's very enthusiastic about my bows."

"So much the better! That's fantastic to meet someone who appreciates your work."

"Yes, it's a good feeling. And you, did he come, the violinist you were expecting?"

"Yes. He has a Vuillaume from 1864! You don't see one of those every day! He'd been banging it around so much with his traveling that it was sorely in need of an adjustment. The young man was very pleased—above all relieved. He has a concert tomorrow evening. His name is Christophe Rubens."

"Ah, yes, I've heard of him. I even heard him play on the radio not that long ago . . . Another rising star!"

"He played the start of the Bach Chaconne on his newly adjusted Vuillaume. It wasn't half bad!"

Jacques Maillard got up and went over to the stereo. He retrieved a CD from a dresser filled with discs and VHS cassettes. A CD player sat on top. He slotted in the disc he'd chosen. Music for a solo violin began to emerge from two little speakers placed close to the ceiling.

"It's the Chaconne, played by Gidon Kremer," murmured Jacques, sitting back down on the sofa.

On hearing the music, Momo awoke and raised her head. Then she jumped onto the sofa to lie down and placed her head on Jacques's lap. The luthier stroked the dog several times, from her head to the base of her curled tail. Momo blinked, relaxing into the luthier's gentle gestures. After a few minutes of musical contemplation, disturbed only by the quiet ticking of the clock and a few sporadic, dreaming sniffles from Momo, Jacques, only just surfacing from a moment of reverie, continued in a tranquil voice: "Before he left, he tried two of my fairly recent violins and, to conclude, my own Vuillaume, playing the Chaconne each time."

The luthier told his companion about the musician's marked preference for the violin that was not for sale. A contented smile lit up Jacques Maillard's face. The Chaconne came to an end.

"I'm so glad your Vuillaume has been appreciated yet again by a high-ranking professional! Would you like some more tea?"

The Prelude of the Partita no. 3, BWV 1006, was beginning.

"Yes, that would be nice, to finish my madeleine. Don't move, Hélène, I'll go put some hot water in the pot. 'Scuse me, Momo, I have to get up . . ."

The dog jumped down from the sofa and lay on the parquet floor. Hélène, for the moment, returned to reading the paper. When Jacques came back with a teapot full of hot water, she said, "I'd love to hear her play, someday, this Midori Yamazaki . . . They speak so highly of her!"

4
.

JACQUES AND HÉLÈNE HAD MET IN MIRECOURT, A LITTLE TOWN in the Vosges that was the French capital of instrument making. They were young then: Jacques only twenty-six, Hélène twenty-one. They had both come to Mirecourt three years earlier.

Jacques was an avid reader, and after his baccalaureate exam, he had spent two years at the Sorbonne to study literature. But he hadn't found what he needed to flourish. The academic approach to literature, by dint of focusing on authorship, seemed to be missing the heart of the matter: a vast field where words resonated to create a work's prime, tangible reality. And so he returned to his childhood dream, of becoming a luthier. Already from early adolescence he had immersed himself in music, as he had in books, in sounds as much as words. His family environment had not been conducive to learning to play the violin or the viola, so he had turned to crafting stringed instruments. It was the best way to engage in the infinite combinations of musical sounds, and in the vast world of deep, diverse emotions that came from them. He decided to go to Mirecourt. He informed his father, who was understanding and told him that the wisest decision would surely be to choose the path that seemed imperative and listen to the voice arising from the source of his vital energy. "Otherwise, your shadow won't follow you. It will be severed from you. After all, you only live once," he asserted, giving a long sigh.

Hélène first came to Mirecourt at the age of sixteen. She had accompanied her parents, both of them professional viola players in Lyon. During one of their trips to the little town in the Vosges to have their respective instruments maintained, they had suggested their daughter go with them. And it was that trip that determined the girl's future. On visiting the workshop of a master bow maker, Hélène was fascinated by his craft. A simple strip of Pernambuco wood was transformed into an object of beauty, and for the first time she saw in its curve—although she had lived every day in such close contact with her parents' bows—a mysterious beauty that made her think of a celestial ship sailing on the silver waves of clouds. Her parents had told her that the sound of their instruments changed markedly depending on the bow; they viewed it as the natural extension of their right arm. Everything took on a new meaning after that. Hélène left Mirecourt promising herself she would come back to learn the art of bow making with a master. She returned two years later with the same determination, which had lost none of its initial intensity, nor its youthful vitality.

Both Hélène and Jacques began their apprenticeships with renowned masters. All their days were alike, peacefully turned out, as if cast from the same mold. They led separate, monastic lives, day after day, wearing a green, navy-blue, or even black apron, cloistered in their dark workshops, speaking little, observing a great deal, all ears, closely watching the way their masters handled their tools, or focusing on their work under the orange light of a desk lamp. When night fell, before going to bed in their modest rooms, where there was hardly the space for a bed and a dresser doing double duty as a table, they would reflect on their day and, occasionally, jot down the essential things they had learned in their books of notes and sketches. Their lives as artisans in a little town of seven thousand souls were eerily similar, like two peas in a pod in their simplicity, regularity, and frugality, in the ardor they put into their work and the repetitive monotony of their everyday life. Yet they had never chanced to meet, to exchange a single gaze, smile, or word. Until, one day, three long years after their arrival in Mirecourt in 1950, they met, as if suddenly guided by a superior intelligence intent on bringing together kindred souls.

Monsieur Laberte, master luthier, sent his apprentice on an errand to Monsieur Bazin, master bow maker. From time to time they would work together for a few clients. The master bow maker's workshop was a ten-minute walk from the workshop of his friend and colleague. It was the first time Jacques had ever been there. He entered the workshop and immediately noticed the master, a man in his fifties with graying hair, thick-lensed glasses, and a round bald patch on top of his head. Jacques handed him a large envelope on his master's behalf. He had said goodbye and was about to leave without further ado. But just as he was going out of the workshop he was struck, on turning back somewhat instinctively, by the presence of a young bespectacled woman at her workbench. She was next to a young apprentice who was scraping a long orangish stick with the help of a tiny plane: long shavings like angel's curls fell bountifully onto the workbench. Jacques had thought, naively until then, that all instrument and bow makers were men. As for the young woman, she was trying to warp a strip of wood ever so gently by heating it above a flame in order to obtain the proper curve. She sensed she was being watched. Raising her head, she saw the young man who stood there, although clearly he had finished his errand as a messenger boy. She smiled at him for a split second before once again focusing on her work. Jacques barely had the time to return her smile. A heavy silence reigned. The only sounds were the constant scraping of the little plane and the rub of the wood strip, from time to time, against the edge of the workbench to obtain the ideal curve.

Jacques turned and left on tiptoe.

That evening, before switching off his bedside lamp, he scribbled a few lines in his green notebook, which bore the number 18 and served as his journal, too, in order to record his unexpected encounter with the mysterious aspiring bow maker.

Switching off the light did not lure Morpheus into Jacques's room. The apprentice lay awake in the dark until late in the night.

5.

DAYS WENT BY, THEN WEEK AFTER WEEK. LIFE WENT BACK TO normal, and nothing came to disturb the two young apprentices' relentless devotion to their work or their calm, obsessive desire to progress in their profession. The very memory of their momentary encounter was soon buried, for both of them, beneath the thick layer of present moments that had accumulated with the passage of time. Neither Jacques nor Hélène thought of the other anymore—and yet, the impression of the smile they'd exchanged did not fossilize at the bottom of the dark well of memory.

One day, however, when they were not restricted by the preoccupations of their professional lives, there was a second encounter. It happened on a radiant sunny afternoon at the end of August. They were both returning to Mirecourt after a short vacation. Jacques had spent his in Normandy, where his father, an only child, had inherited the family home. As for the apprentice bow maker, she had just rested and found peace of mind in the countryside, at her parents' holiday home not far from Dijon. They alighted from the train and walked with their packs on their backs toward the station hall. Their eyes met. There were few other travelers; this made their mutual recognition easier.

"Hello!"

"Hello, do you remember me?"

"Yes, I can't remember when it was, but you came one time to the workshop."

"That's right. Well, what a surprise! We were on the same train, if I'm not mistaken."

"Apparently. Have you just been on vacation?"

"Yes. You, too?"

"Yes."

They agreed to stop at a café. They searched for a quiet place. After walking for a few minutes, they sat down under a parasol on a restaurant terrace.

"My name's Hélène, Hélène Becker," said the bow maker, holding her hand out to the luthier.

"Jacques Maillard. How long have you been in Mirecourt?"

"Three and a half years. I'm originally from the Hérault, but my family lives in Lyon. And you?"

"I'm from Paris. Well, it's not quite that simple, but I can say, more or less, that I've always lived in Paris. I arrived in Mirecourt a little over three years ago, too . . ."

The waiter came to take their order, and they both asked for coffee.

"When I saw you in Monsieur Bazin's workshop, I was really surprised, because I thought—wrongly, it seems—that there were no women in this profession . . ."

"You're right, it's almost always been the exclusive domain of men. It took Monsieur Bazin quite a while to accept me . . ."

The conversation grew lively. Initially they spoke of the joys and difficulties of their craft. Hélène shared with Jacques the happiness she felt when she managed to apply the ideal curve to a simple strip of Pernambuco that had been revived from several decades of sleep for drying.

"Pernambuco—is that the famous wood that was introduced by a great French master in the eighteenth century? Uh, François . . . ?"

"François Xavier Tourte."

"Yes, that's it."

"It's a tree that grows only in Brazil. I think it's extraordinary that in order to perfect his art he thought of a tree that grows so far away. Don't you agree?"

"Yes, it's extraordinary . . . It's his passion that took him all that way, technically and geographically."

Jacques, in turn, spoke of his admiration for the great master luthiers, from the time of Amati, who established a lasting standard for the various woods to be used in making stringed instruments: spruce for the soundboard; maple for the bottom, the neck, the ribs, and the bridge; ebony for the fingerboard and tailpiece. Like Hélène, he worked with wood that had been allowed to dry naturally over a long period of time, and he was fascinated—just as she was—by the beauty of the curve of a bow, by the graceful elegance of the arch that had to be shaped both on the back and on the soundboard in order to give the instrument its supernatural ability to vibrate. Perfect mastery of the appropriate tool for each maneuver had to be acquired until it became muscle memory. It required constant effort and boundless patience. But he was never discouraged. On the contrary, he merely tried harder, convincing himself that a magnificent, splendid sound would await him at the end of this long path.

They looked at each other and marveled deeply at the way chance, or the exigency of fate, had brought them to this town in the Vosges to be initiated into the mysteries of the production of musical sound.

"I'm only just beginning my adventure," Jacques concluded, his tone lucid and hopeful.

"Likewise," answered Hélène.

Time had been ticking by, under the café parasol, without the two young artisans noticing how quickly and silently it had passed. The sun was already beginning to set. It was time to go, for them to head to their respective workshops. They promised to meet again. They shook hands and parted. Their forms vanished into the growing darkness of the narrow streets.

6.

TWO MORE YEARS WENT BY, WITH THE ROUTINE OF REGULARLY resumed observations, the imperturbable tranquility of constantly renewed reflections, and the love of gestures relentlessly repeated day after day. What had changed, in comparison to the first three years, when Jacques and Hélène did not yet know each other, though they lived and worked in such close proximity, was that they began to meet regularly, a routine gradually established after their unexpected encounter at the station. At first, they saw each other every two or three weeks, but before long, more frequently—on a weekly basis. They often got together for a quick bite during their noontime break. In the evenings, after work was done, they sometimes dined, just the two of them, at a dark, dingy restaurant, where they would linger until late at night. Words came from one heart only to go deep into the other. Then, remembering that the next day would be just as demanding as the previous ones, they said good night and returned to their lodgings to rest their tired eyes and revive the tense muscles in their arms and shoulders during a brief but substantial sleep, often visited by dreams of the future. There was a solidarity between them; they could open their hearts in each other's presence, and they found they shared a philosophy where personal accomplishment was intimately connected to the patiently sought perfection of their art. Their individual worlds were being enhanced, enriched, enlarged, too, through the time they spent together and what they exchanged.

One day, heartfelt words slipped from Hélène's lips: "Someday, maybe someone will play one of your violins using one of my bows!"

And she blushed bright red.

"Why not?" said Jacques, his tone almost dreamy, as he gazed into the bow maker's eyes.

Hélène wrote to her parents on a regular basis. They replied quickly. They gave her their news, and news of family and friends. In this way Hélène found out who, among her former classmates, had *found a husband*, and who was engaged. She realized that the years were passing and that she, too, had reached an age when marriage was on most young women's minds. In her bed, before nodding off, she would envisage her future, sometimes with a dull, persistent anxiety: that future had not yet taken a precise shape and might persist for a long time in this unstable haze. Even in the middle of the day, in her master's workshop, she was startled to find herself daydreaming, imagining herself in a family and professional environment that would bring her happiness and satisfaction. And deep down she could not help but picture her life merging with Jacques's . . .

Until one rainy spring day, when she was confronted with something totally unexpected. Jacques invited her to dinner the following Sunday in a *real restaurant*. They'd always made do with a brasserie in town that was hardly better than a school cafeteria. Jacques insisted their meeting that Sunday should take place in a different environment.

"Let me—I'll take care of everything!" said Jacques.

Wearing a jacket and tie, Jacques went to fetch Hélène at the workshop of Master Bazin, who provided her lodgings. The young woman was lightly made up, wearing a light green dress. The young man was surprised by Hélène's discreet beauty: he had never really noticed it before, when she wore her bow maker's apron. They took the train to Épinal and went into a restaurant called Au Buisson Ardent near the station. Once they had ordered, there was a moment of silence where each seemed to be probing the other's expectancy, to be guessing at the words that, in the other's consciousness, were about to be formulated, combined, spoken.

"It's a special day today," said Hélène at last.

Jacques thought she must be wanting to encourage him to whisper a few sweet nothings in her ear. He forced himself not to yield to her silent appeal; although his heart heard it perfectly, his will refused to respond.

"Yes, it's a special day . . . I've come to an important decision."

"Oh, really?" murmured Hélène, impatient.

"Yes, well . . . how to put it . . . I've decided to leave Mirecourt."

Hélène was stunned and could not say a word.

"I—I'm—I'm going to continue my training in Cremona. Monsieur Laberte put me in touch with a great master there, who has agreed to take me on. I still have so much to learn, particularly with regard to restoration."

"I thought—" Hélène struggled against a wave of emotion. "I thought we'd go on for a long time like this . . ."

Hélène was doing all she could not to break down. Jacques, disturbed by the sudden display of emotion, which to some degree he had expected but not with this intensity, tried to remain calm while he explained, unhurriedly, the reasons behind his decision.

"I, too, would have liked things to go on the way they have . . . But it's impossible. I have to tell you something important, Hélène."

The young bow maker, who had lowered her head to shield her tears, now glanced up and ran her right hand over her cheeks.

"I've never spoken about any of this with you . . . but I've had a plan for a long time. The five years I've spent in Mirecourt are in fact only the first stage . . . Forgive me, I should have mentioned it to you sooner, but it was hard. In the beginning I went through a period when I was indecisive and wondered if I was really cut out for this trade, if it was really worth persevering . . . Then, once I'd managed to put my doubts behind me, I began to dream of my future as a luthier, alongside your own . . . Like you, maybe . . . But I can't give up on the plans I've been nurturing ever since, I guess, my childhood. We came to this restaurant because I want to tell you about my plan . . . It will take a while."

Hélène's face, gradually regaining its calm, now seemed to indicate that her heart was ready to hear the young luthier's explanation, to find out why what he had learned in Mirecourt thus far could no longer satisfy him.

"So, where to begin?" wondered Jacques.

The waiter brought them their meals.

"Bon appétit."

"Thank you. Bon appétit to you, too."

"Thanks. Hélène, I've often wanted to ask you if you never wondered why I have a typically French name, despite my Asian features . . ."

"In the beginning, I did. I figured you must be from a family who were originally Vietnamese or Chinese, and since you were born in France, they gave you a French name. I didn't take it any further. In any case, it never bothered me! I've never given much thought to people's looks, or their names, or where they're from. What matters is who you become, through your own efforts, your will . . . Don't you think?"

"My name is Jacques Maillard, but I'm also called, or rather, I used to be called Rei Mizusawa. I *was* Japanese. I ended up orphaned in Tokyo and was adopted by Monsieur and Madame Maillard, who raised me as their son . . ."

And so Jacques began to tell the story of what he had lived through, almost twenty years earlier, how he had spent most of an afternoon trembling with fear in the solitary darkness of a European wardrobe, in a corner of a meeting room in a house of culture somewhere in the vastness of Tokyo. Driven by a desire to re-create as faithfully as possible the scene he had witnessed through the keyhole in the wardrobe, he hardly touched his food. As for Hélène, she was eating just as slowly, captivated by the story her friend the luthier recounted. The lunch seemed to go on forever. In the end, by the time Jacques had finally finished his life story, they were alone at Au Buisson Ardent. They hadn't had dessert yet.

"I'm not hungry anymore," said Hélène.

"Neither am I. Maybe we should get going, it's nearly time for the train."

Jacques paid the bill, thanked the waiter, and apologized for taking so long. Then they left.

"Darn, it's raining," whispered Hélène.

"Il pleut sur la ville comme il pleure dans mon coeur . . ."

"You've got it the wrong way round."

"Yes, I know. But that's just how it came to me."

Back in Mirecourt, they walked slowly toward Monsieur Bazin's workshop.

"When will you leave for Cremona?"

"In two weeks. We still have time to see each other."

"Will you stay there long?"

"I don't know."

"Will we write to each other?"

"Yes, of course. We'll write. I'll write to you regularly."

Despite the fact that they were walking as slowly as possible, as if to delay for as long as possible the moment when they must say good night and goodbye, they arrived at Monsieur Bazin's too quickly. Neither one of them had been able to do a thing to prolong their time together. The only light came from a ghostly street lamp. Hélène thanked Jacques for the restaurant and, above all, for his life story, which had moved her deeply. Jacques thanked Hélène for her pleasant company, the attentive, understanding way she listened. Then he added how precious her tender, sweet, close, kindly, comforting *friendship* was to him. He took her hand and kissed it. They looked at each other. Hélène thought that, through Jacques's glasses, as they reflected the pale ambient glow, she could see his eyes sparkling under a thin veil of tears. Their faces drew closer; they kissed for the first time. Their embrace was long and passionate. Finally, they parted. Hélène stood motionless outside her workshop until her friend's shadow had disappeared into the darkness of the next street.

7.

ONE WINTER EVENING HÉLÈNE CAME HOME, VISIBLY AGITATED, and turned to Jacques, who was sitting on the living room sofa reading, with Momo at his feet.

"Look what I found, Jacques. Do you remember, two or three years ago, I showed you a short paragraph in *Libé* about Midori Yamazaki, the Japanese violinist? My curiosity was piqued by what she said about her grandfather's decisive influence regarding her career as a musician."

"Yes. It was when she won first prize . . . I've forgotten now, some competition . . ."

"Read this, it's an interview she gave recently to *Music and Words*. She says her grandfather had been an officer in the army, but that hadn't stopped him from nurturing a deep love of music. She says, 'It is thanks to my grandfather that I have become who I am today . . . I owe as much, if not more, to him, as to my professor, Madame Suzuki.'"

Jacques, immersed in a tiny Japanese book, looked up and reached for the magazine.

"'I am what I learned from my grandfather.'"

After reading the title out loud, he read the entire article in silence.

"Yes, indeed, a twenty-six-year-old violinist talking about her grandfather the former officer in these terms . . . I agree there are some intriguing clues. It might be worth looking into."

"That's what I was thinking, too. If you wrote to her—"

"But how?"

"Send a letter to her agent. Normally they forward everything they get to the artist."

Jacques didn't react to what Hélène said; he was lost to an abyss of sad thoughts and aching memories. He picked up his Japanese book, which was lying open, facedown. It was a book with countless Post-its, making one think of the multicolored strands of hair that sprout from a cartoon character's head. The book was carefully protected by a brown paper wrapper, very worn from constant handling, and the cover was inscribed in black felt-tip pen with two ideograms and eight letters in hiragana.

8
.

BECAUSE HE HAD COME TO FRANCE AT THE AGE OF ELEVEN AND
had immediately enrolled in the French school system, Rei
had fallen out of the habit of speaking Japanese. He had even,
temporarily, lost the ability to read and write his mother
tongue. Now that he was transplanted into a French context,
every effort the boy made would consist primarily in learning
the language of his host country. Philippe, true to the memory
of his lost friend Yu Mizusawa, provided his adoptive son with
kindly affection and tender love. He made sure the child who
had been so brutally deprived of a father would grow up in
as healthy an environment as possible, although he knew
that the wound inflicted on the child's heart would remain
open for a long time all the same—if not forever—and that it
would probably never heal. As for his wife, Isabelle, because
she knew she could not have children, she gave her love to
the Japanese boy and found ample justification in him for her
maternal love.

Philippe and Isabelle Maillard wanted their adoptive son to
spend the later years of his childhood and adolescence in harmony with his new surroundings, or in any case as unevent-
fully as possible, with a minimum of psychological conflict.
This was why, after consulting a psychologist, they gave Rei,

who had never wanted to part with his father's ruined violin, the name Jacques, in honor of the greatest French violinist of their era, Jacques Thibaud.

"Now, in addition to the fine name Rei that your *otōsan*, your father, gave you, you have the French name Jacques. Your new name won't erase your Japanese one, which means 'politeness and courtesy,' if I remember correctly what your *otōsan* told me one day. Isn't that right? The two names will mutually reinforce each other. This way you'll be twice as strong! Here in France, your new country, I'll be standing in for your *otōsan*. I have such wonderful memories of him. I will try to live up to him."

It was in these terms that Philippe spoke to Rei one day, in French, using the odd Japanese expression here and there to make sure he would be understood. In six months of school the boy had attained a level of oral comprehension that was reassuring.

From then on, with the love and protection of his French parents, which enabled him to overcome as best he could the fear—concealed, unspoken, repressed—that he carried deep in his heart, Jacques made dazzling progress in French, so much so that a few years later he was one of the top pupils in class. And it was then that the desire to keep close something of his vanished father's language gradually returned. He opened *How Do You Live?* by Genzaburo Yoshino, the very book his father had recommended to him, that he had been reading—he now remembered with sorrow, as if emerging from a nightmare—on the day of the tragedy that had taken his father from him, ruthlessly and forever. He read Yoshino's book over and over, tirelessly. In a school notebook, in green ink, he copied out the words he liked, phrases that rang pleasantly in his ear, and even, on occasion, entire pages he felt like underlining. Since he had no one to speak Japanese with, Jacques had gotten into the habit of writing it. And so his green notebook became first and foremost a secret garden, where things grew back, resurfaced, things he'd left behind in Tokyo, the fragments of which he had stored in a remote, obscure region of his child's soul. It was only later, when he was fifteen or so, and the habit of writing in his journal had become deeply ingrained, like a remedy for his obsessive fear, that Jacques began to write in French as well. And so, in his succession of green notebooks—every year, he invariably bought a green pupil's notebook for the purpose—the pages in French were scattered with Japanese writing, with hiragana and ideograms of varying complexity.

9.

THE DAY JACQUES DECIDED TO WRITE TO MIDORI YAMAZAKI, HE did not, therefore, have much difficulty writing in Japanese. Naturally he could write more fluently in French, but to express himself in Japanese was not a major obstacle. In all likelihood he did not write like a native who had always resided in Japan. His active knowledge of ideograms was limited. Because he had become French and spent six-sevenths of his life in France, his use of Japanese was like that of a foreigner. But while the necessity of communicating in Japanese did require a particular effort, it did not, for all that, come at a price. Jacques knew that the violinist had been living in France to complete her studies at the Conservatoire de Paris; she would certainly understand French. And yet he still chose Japanese. What he had to say was something that touched the deepest level of his identity, the *event* in his life that he had experienced sixty-five years earlier in Japanese, but which had been frozen, fixed, or petrified since then, as if time had been slain and had coagulated, coming to a halt for good.

One Thursday evening Jacques taped a sheet of white paper to the front door, on which he had written, "Closed Due to Exceptional Circumstances." The following morning, after breakfast, Rei began writing the first draft of his letter in his green notebook, which was now numbered 65. He wrote three pages without stopping. He read them over. He wanted to tweak a few sentences, substitute some words for others—more precise, appropriate—then completely rewrite two or three poorly constructed paragraphs. On Saturday morning, he returned to his draft, and when he felt he'd gotten as far as he could with his missive, the winter sun was already setting. Hélène told him to get some rest. They decided they would make themselves a pot of matcha.

"So, have you finished?"

"Yes, nearly. It's probably not very well written. There are bound to be mistakes or awkward turns of phrase; there are few ideograms because I simply don't know all that many. A lot of the words are in hiragana, starting with the names of individuals like Lieutenant Kurokami. But in the end I think I've gotten the important points across. I'll stop there. I'll read it again tomorrow. And if it's good, I'll make a final clean copy."

That night Jacques had difficulty getting to sleep. Hélène noticed.

They caressed each other for a long time under the comforter before drifting off, united in sleep, nestled together.

10
.

AFTER WAITING ROUGHLY A WEEK THAT SEEMED INTERMINABLE, Rei received an email from Midori Yamazaki. Like an X-ray, it shot through the entire stratum of lost time.

From: Midori Yamazaki
To: 水澤礼 / Rei Mizusawa / Jacques Maillard
Subject: Thank you very much for your letter.
Date: February 28, 2003

Dear Monsieur Maillard,

Thank you very much for your letter, which has left me amazed and astonished.

Indeed, my maternal grandfather was called Kengo Kurokami. He was a lieutenant in the army. So he is the man you saw in 1938, in such dramatic circumstances. He departed this world in 1993.

I would be very happy to meet with you. Just now, however, I am about to go on tour in the US and Canada for three weeks. I will be in touch when I get back. And we shall try to arrange something so that we can meet.

Thank you very much for writing. I have been deeply moved to hear from you.

Kindest regards,
Midori Yamazaki

The message was written in a simple, limpid Japanese that Rei had no difficulty understanding. The grandfather's first and last name were written in hiragana, as in Rei's own letter. Was this an indication of her tactful consideration, an effort to share the auditory perceptions of the child Rei? Or had she, by placing herself in the shoes of the strange author of that extraordinary letter, been thinking, rather, of the particularly difficult circumstances a person would find himself in, having lost the use of his native tongue after being brutally wrenched from his childhood? Rei felt something like a burning in his stomach, an acid heat both intense and diffuse welling in his throat. An enormous block of frozen emotions gradually began to melt upon impact with this dormant inner heat. It was like an American black bear slowly rousing itself from hibernation and becoming increasingly active as the eagerly awaited spring approached.

Time was emerging from its fossilized state, beginning to quiver.

III

MENUETTO: ALLEGRETTO

1
.

"HELLO. REI MIZUSAWA."

"Hello. I've been expecting you. Please come in."

With both hands, Rei Mizusawa gave Midori Yamazaki a business card he had prepared for his trip to Tokyo. The violinist glanced at it. "So, Jacques Maillard is your French name, if I've understood correctly."

"Yes, that's right. I work with both names. Thank you for agreeing to see me . . ."

Rei was standing in the entrance. On the parquet floor, raised roughly eight inches higher than the vestibule, a pair of white slippers pointed toward the interior of the living space.

"Those are for you," said Midori.

The young Japanese woman gave a warm, welcoming smile as she indicated the slippers. Her French guest sat down on the edge of the parquet to remove his sneakers, which he then left side by side on the tiled floor of the vestibule.

He was ushered into a large room where two walls were covered from top to bottom with books and musical scores. In the middle stood a grand piano, and next to it, a sofa and two armchairs the color of daffodils.

"Have a seat; make yourself at home."

Rei set his leather briefcase on the floor, alongside a burgundy violin case that was worn like a backpack. Someone knocked on the door. A woman in her fifties entered, wrapped in a kimono, carrying a round tray with three cups of tea.

"My mother."

"Very nice to meet you. My name is Ayako Yamazaki. My daughter has told me so much about you and your letter. She had me read it as well. I've been greatly looking forward to meeting you."

"Ah, that lovely smell of *genmaicha*! Thank you very much."

"You know it?" asked Mrs. Yamazaki, sounding somewhat surprised.

"Yes, my companion and I drink a lot of tea . . . including *genmaicha*."

"If I remember correctly, from your letter, you haven't been back to Japan since . . . ?" asked Midori.

"No, this is the first time. I've been away for sixty-five years. I'm seventy-six. I'm an old man now."

"So, you were eleven, when it happened . . ."

"Yes."

"And you've been living in France ever since?"

"Yes, I was adopted by a French friend of my father's. I grew up in France."

"But it's astonishing," said Mrs. Yamazaki, "that you speak Japanese so naturally, even though you haven't lived here in such a long time."

"Oh, no, madam, the way I speak must be rather strange . . ."

"One can tell you're from *somewhere else*. But it doesn't keep us from communicating at all."

"My spoken Japanese froze, so to speak, when I stopped living in Japan. But I did go on reading . . . I read a great deal.

No doubt my reading has helped me maintain my Japanese. Later, once I became a luthier, I eventually got to know quite a few Japanese musicians, which has given me the opportunity to speak the language fairly often." Rei spoke slowly, his voice deep, his tone calm and confident, with the occasional pause. "So, you are the granddaughter of Lieutenant Kurokami."

"I am."

Suddenly speechless, the elderly French visitor had to catch his breath before continuing the conversation.

"I would never have imagined I might meet his granddaughter someday. Just think."

"You have had quite an extraordinary life, all the same," said Ayako Yamazaki, her tone full of wonder.

"Tell me about your father, your grandfather. You know, my encounter with him was so fleeting, wordless . . . It lasted only a few seconds, half a minute. But I can recall perfectly the hesitant smile he gave me as he handed me my father's ruined violin. After everyone had left—my father, his friends, and the soldiers—only your grandfather remained. And just then someone called to him, shouting his name. It sounded to me like Kurokami. And I remembered it easily. It was etched in my memory, once and for all, in indelible letters, associated with the idea of black hair . . ."

The young musician was looking at her mother with a smiling, mysterious air, as if encouraging her to speak.

"In fact, Kurokami means 'black god,' not 'black hair,'" said Mrs. Yamazaki.

"Oh, really? Kami is the *kami* in *god*? Well, I'll be!" said Rei, flabbergasted.

"It's a very rare name. It's in the prefecture of Hiroshima, apparently, that you will find the greatest concentration of Kurokami. And my father was from Hiroshima."

"You must have heard of Miyajima," added Midori. "It's a well-known tourist site, with a large torii gate in the sea. Well, beyond that island, with all its visitors, there's another one that's uninhabited, and it's called 'the island of the Great Black God.'"

"I was sure it meant 'black hair.' I never thought for a second that it could mean 'black god.' That's normal when you don't know, I think: the combination of 'black' and 'god' is fairly unlikely, don't you agree? In any case, it was not something I would have expected. If I'd known, I would have been even more surprised, for sure."

"It rather upends the image you had of my grandfather."

"It does indeed! Incredible . . . The man I saw briefly from the gloom of my wardrobe hiding place was therefore a *Black God!*" cried Rei, leaving off his usual calm manner. "A *God* in the *Darkness*, a *God* who rose from *Blackest* obscurity, the place of nightmares . . ."

Then he murmured something. He was speaking to himself.

"I was saved by him. Like my father's violin, actually."

Then he fell silent.

He was staring into space.

2.

IT WAS A FINE DAY IN MAY, OF WHICH THERE ARE FEW IN TOKYO—
days that are neither too hot nor too cold, with no humidity,
bathed in a bright light, decked in lush vegetation, lulled by a
breeze as light as a caress. Rei had arrived at Midori Yamazaki's
house at around ten thirty. The French visitor and his two
hostesses lingered over the lieutenant's name and the evocative power of the ideograms depicting Japanese names. The
time passed, and they did not notice. It was almost noon.

"You're not in a hurry, I hope, Mr. Mizusawa. You'll stay
and have lunch with us. We are free all day today. We want to
spend the day with you, if it's not a bother."

"With pleasure, madam. I came to Japan solely to meet you.
I have nothing else to do."

"Well, then, I will leave you both and go to the kitchen to
see to lunch. It's nearly ready. It will take me fifteen minutes
or so. I'll be right back."

After a moment of silence, Rei was the first to speak. "I wrote
in my letter that it was the interview you gave to *Music and
Words* that originally compelled me to write you . . ."

"Yes. What you noted was what I'd been saying about my
grandfather—wasn't that it? 'I am what I learned from my
grandfather.'"

"Yes, that's it, it was the title of the interview. And what was decisive was the fact that your grandfather had been an officer in the army. So when I saw that, I could not get it out of my mind."

"I see."

"In fact, it was my companion, Hélène, who had this incredible hunch. She is a bow maker, and of course she knows my story."

"Your wife is a bow maker! That's incredible—what a perfect match, like a violin and its bow!"

"Yes, if you like. We were apprenticed at the same time."

"Where?"

"In a small town called Mirecourt, in Lorraine—"

"Mirecourt! I've been there!" cried Midori.

"You have? Oh, we were there so long ago . . ."

The luthier fell silent for a few moments. Then he continued: "From the very first signs, Hélène was sensitive to the secret, invisible connection I would have with you. For example, when you won first prize at the Ludwig van Beethoven International Violin Competition, she showed me a little article about you that she found in *Libération*. What stood out, for her, was precisely the fact that you stressed your grandfather's role in your education."

Mrs. Yamazaki came back into the room. "Lunch is served!"

The dining room was at the far end of the corridor. Rei followed Midori, who was speaking to her mother, her voice full of emotion: "His wife is a bow maker—they studied together in Mirecourt!"

"Mirecourt! I can't believe it," answered Ayako, in a small voice.

They were in a living room that opened onto the kitchen. On the large rectangular table, which could easily seat eight people, three places were set.

"I've made something very simple, homestyle cooking of the type you probably don't get a chance to eat in France. Breaded pork with finely shredded cabbage . . ."

"Ah, it's *tonkatsu*! With *misoshiru*! It's been so long since I had this . . ."

"But you have Japanese restaurants in Paris . . ."

"Yes, of course. But that's just the thing, there aren't that many that do homestyle cooking. And even if there were, we couldn't go every day. You know, I left Japan so long ago that Japanese food is really not something I eat every day. So you cannot imagine the huge pleasure this gives me!"

"It's really not much, Mr. Mizusawa . . ."

"*Itadakimasu*," said Rei, bowing slightly, and instinctively putting his hands together.

Midori and her mother echoed him, in unison.

"Do you say grace before you eat?" Midori asked.

"No, why? I'm not religious . . ."

"Because you made that gesture," said Midori, joining her hands in turn.

"Oh, did I? That's strange, I never do so when I eat at home."

The two women didn't know what to say.

"Well, this is absolutely delicious, Mrs. Yamazaki!" exclaimed Rei, after his first sip of the miso.

"Thank you. I'm glad you like it. It's really not much, you know."

A silence came over them. Midori glanced furtively at the luthier.

Rei had just taken his first small bite of the breaded pork. Then he poured a little soy sauce onto a *tsukemono*, a fine slice of cucumber macerated in salt. When he had placed the oval piece in his mouth, time sent him back, uncontrollably, to the eleven-year-old Rei Mizusawa he had once been, eating his breakfast one autumn morning in 1938. He had sat on the tatami at a little round table across from his father. He departed the company of the two women, to be led down the well of his distant memory. His father appeared before him in his kitchen apron, busy making little things for them to eat. Suddenly Rei turned and said to Ayako Yamazaki: "May I have an egg?"

"An egg?"

"Yes, an egg. Forgive me, it's very impolite of me . . ."

Rei went on, like a sleepwalker. "I think I ate a *namatamago* that day, a raw egg . . . The urge has suddenly come over me, to pour a raw egg, beaten and mixed with soy sauce, over this nice hot rice . . . It's as if this delicious rice, along with the taste of *tsukemono*, has abruptly spirited me into the darkness of my childhood years ago. Yes, that morning, I had a *namatamago* for breakfast, that Sunday in 1938, the day my father disappeared."

Rei was muttering to himself, mindless of the two women's presence. It seemed to Midori that the old man's body was possessed by someone else. Her mother, intrigued and even a little concerned, returned from the kitchen with an egg sitting in a little porcelain bowl, in its white shell.

3.

REI BROKE THE EGG AND BEAT IT ENERGETICALLY. THEN HE added the equivalent of a little spoonful of soy sauce. Finally, he poured it all onto his rice, mixing it with his chopsticks.

Midori and her mother watched the elderly child eating his rice with raw egg. It seemed a profane liturgy unfolded before their eyes, one in which they were unable to take part.

"Does this remind you of anything?" Midori asked her mother.

"Of course it does."

"Thank you very much," said Rei, his tone confident, as if he had just woken from a dream.

"Has it been a long time since you had rice with raw egg?"

"Yes, a very long time. This is surely the first time since breakfast that day with my father. Excuse me for being so impolite. It was as if I could feel a cold hand at my back, a trembling hand pushing me, taking me elsewhere. And I let it . . ."

"Please, don't worry about it, Mr. Mizusawa," answered Ayako Yamazaki, looking at her daughter.

It was Midori's turn to say, "I think I understand what happened to you when you relived these tastes you had known as a child, that you lost during your years in France. And, without realizing it, you also reminded me of my grandfather, during your little journey away from the present."

"What do you mean?"

"I'll let my mother explain, because she was reminded of her father . . . too . . . when she saw you magically reconnect with your eleven-year-old self, in Tokyo."

And so, Ayako Yamazaki began to recount the story of a trip to Europe Kengo Kurokami had absolutely insisted on taking, when he was eighty-nine years old.

"My father had been widowed for four years, and no doubt he was sensing his oncoming death. But that didn't stop him from setting off on his first, and last, trip abroad. He told me what he would like to do. I spoke to my husband, who whole-heartedly embraced his father-in-law's plan. I think my father wanted to show his twelve-year-old granddaughter the birthplace of the music she studied every day. With the support, therefore, of his daughter and son-in-law, Kengo Kurokami, my father, or your Black God, found the strength, despite advanced age, to make a two-week trip to Europe in 1987. We visited several European cities, where music played a significant role in collective memory: first to Berlin, then from Berlin to Prague, from Prague to Vienna, from Vienna to Milan, and then Cremona, where we admired the Museo del Violino. After the Italian capital of instrument making, we actually did go to Mirecourt, for two days, before returning to Tokyo. He insisted we go to Mirecourt after Cremona. My husband and I only knew of Cremona . . . 'Isn't Cremona enough for you, where instrument making is concerned?' I asked. No, we absolutely had to go to Mirecourt!

"Midori and I, on seeing you with your raw egg, felt a

memory awaken in our hearts of an event that actually took place in Mirecourt. My father, after over ten days of eating European food, had become disgusted by restaurant meals. He couldn't eat another bite. And yet he had to eat something. We went to the only Chinese restaurant in the town. I ordered him a noodle soup, thinking it might be closer to what he was used to. He had never known anything other than the light, simple cuisine of his homeland. Even the noodle soup wouldn't go down. At that point my father himself addressed the waiter, in a French that was halting at best: 'Um . . . white . . . rice and . . . um . . . one egg, please . . .'

"Astonished by this very odd request, the waiter asked my father: 'How would you like your egg, monsieur?'

"'One egg! Like that. One egg!'

"Just then, my husband, who had grasped what his father-in-law meant to do from the start, started speaking in English to explain that he simply wanted a raw egg. After two or three minutes had passed, the kindly waiter brought a bowl of rice and a white egg, setting them down in front of his strange customer. Intrigued, the chef in his toque came out to have a look at the old man. The chef's presence attracted the attention of other customers at nearby tables. The waiter, the chef, the customers—everyone wondered what the elderly Japanese man was going to do with his unusual order. Then he murmured a few words to my husband. A bit embarrassed, my husband asked the waiter to bring a little bowl for his father-in-law.

"The waiter disappeared, then returned at once with an empty bowl, which he handed to the old man.

"'Thank you very much, monsieur!'

"My father broke the egg into the bowl and energetically beat it with his chopsticks. He took the bottle of soy sauce and added a few drops, then stirred some more. Then he poured the yellow and brown mixture over the rice. He murmured a few words I couldn't make out. Finally, in the space of a few minutes he had eaten his bowl of rice with the beaten raw egg seasoned with soy sauce. Once he'd finished his improvised dinner, he put both hands together and bowed slightly. The chef went back to the kitchen; the waiter resumed his usual to-and-fro; the customers turned their attention back to their food or to their order. Our own dinner was brought to us. Then Midori asked her grandfather, 'Was it good, Grandfather?'

"'Ah, yes, Midori-chan, my little Midori.'

"'It looks like it's the first time you've eaten something good since we left Tokyo!'

"'Well, I think you're right. This is the first time I've enjoyed my food since we got to Europe. You know, Midori, I'm an old man. All these good things, in these countries you've seen, they don't agree with my stomach anymore. But I'm not sorry to be here with you, even if I suffered a little because of the food. I'm not sorry at all. On the contrary, I'm very glad that I've seen Europe with you. Because the music you're studying was born here. And we saw the violins in Cremona, and here in Mirecourt! It's wonderful, these people who make violins and bows. For music to reach us, we need composers to create music. We need performers, instrumentalists—violinists, for example, who play the music—but we also need the people who make their instruments, their violins and their bows. It takes the participation of these three categories . . . um . . .

these three groups of people. Otherwise, there's no music, you see. Isn't that wonderful? Don't forget that, Midori-chan. I will certainly remember Mirecourt for a very long time.'

"The next morning we left the little town in Lorraine for Paris, where we were scheduled to attend a concert with Yehudi Menuhin playing Beethoven's Concerto for Violin and Orchestra."

Rei gave a start when he heard the name Menuhin.

He looked at the two women.

Recalling the scene at the Chinese restaurant, he tried to imagine the emotion that must have filled the heart of the elderly gentleman who had come halfway around the world to the town of Jean-Baptiste and Nicolas François Vuillaume to show it to his granddaughter. Now Rei was shaken by a dark silent force, rising up from his guts. Why had the Black God decided to go to Mirecourt, such a little-known place, so slight in comparison to Cremona? Could his father have told him, that day, that his violin had been made by Nicolas François Vuillaume of Mirecourt? Rei's mind darted from one question to the next, one conjecture to the next, one supposition to the next. Struggling with so much uncertainty, he became upset. He was only too aware that every heart on earth, isolated in unquiet solitude, was akin to an impenetrable monad, turned in on itself. And that in the end every heart on earth was like every body, separated from every other body, all so painfully foreign to each other.

4
.

THEY HAD JUST FINISHED THEIR MEAL. AYAKO MADE SOME green tea and served it in three irregular rustic cups.

"These cups were made by a friend who's a potter, living out in the sticks, in Tohoku. We like them a lot."

"They're lovely, very pleasing indeed."

"He's a person who is entirely devoted to the pursuit of beauty in his pottery," Ayako continued. "He creates his pottery with absolutely no thought of selling it. Of course, he produces the odd little things he needs to make a living, teacups or flower vases, for example. He makes just enough to survive. The rest of his time and energy is strictly reserved for the endless process of perfecting his art. He's radical and will make no concessions in that respect. These cups were a gift."

"I think I understand your friend. When you feel as if you've really succeeded in doing something, you don't want it to become part of some business transaction. I rarely get the feeling I've perfected anything. But it has happened, once or twice . . . Regarding Mr. Kurokami, I would like to ask you a few questions."

"Fine, but I'm not sure I'll be able to answer. He wasn't a talkative man; he didn't talk about himself. My mother often said, 'Why doesn't he speak? It's no fun living with someone who doesn't speak!' The little I know about my father's past came from my mother, not from him."

"Oh, really? So was he a rather gloomy, melancholic person?"

"Yes. Completely. My mother complained about his withdrawn, uncommunicative nature, but she also said, 'You have to understand him. His entire family was killed in Hiroshima by that horrendous mushroom cloud.'"

"His entire family!"

"Yes—his parents, grandparents, his sister and her husband, their children, his younger brother . . . all burned to death. He was an officer in the army. He lived in Tokyo. So he escaped the catastrophe. A few days after that fateful day of August 6, he went to Hiroshima. And there, of course, he saw the horror. He never got over it . . . He never spoke about it."

"The war ended in August 1945. What became of him after that? The army was finished. What sort of work did he do?"

"He found work as an engineer in a nickel production company. He stayed there until his retirement. According to my mother, he did try, once, to get a position with a publisher that specialized in classical music, but to no avail."

"When did he get married?"

"In 1946. And I was born in 1948."

"Mr. Kurokami was a great music lover, wasn't he? What sort of music in particular? What were his preferences?"

"He loved Mozart and Beethoven. But he was also interested in other periods. Let's say he enjoyed listening to Monteverdi as much as Shostakovich. His favorites among the twentieth-century composers were Bartók and Berg. He greatly admired

Berg's violin concerto, *To the Memory of an Angel,* and his opera, *Wozzeck.* He used to say, 'I hope Midori will play this concerto someday.'"

"But—" Midori interrupted her mother. "More than anything he loved string quartets. Particularly the ones by Mozart, Beethoven, and Schubert. I remember what he told me one day: 'This is the exact opposite of what I hate most: military music.'"

"Music in the army?"

"Yes. The music that was used to 'transform soldiers into herds of cattle,' as he put it. This military music that he couldn't help but hear in the army was, to him, a corruption of music. Instead of being a place for an inner, private experience, 'military music stripped man of his individual essence.' Those were his very words. He despised military music. I think he needed to immerse himself in music to erase any trace of that depraved rhythm within himself."

"Perhaps he was seeking refuge in the solitude of music," said Rei, "in order to oppose the collective enthusiasm that military music perpetuated and reinforced."

"Precisely. When he would come home from work in the evening, the first thing he did was to put a record on: he'd listen to quartets—the six quartets Mozart dedicated to Haydn, or Beethoven's last quartets. He regularly went through a period when he would listen obsessively to *Rosamunde* and *Death and the Maiden.* He also loved Bach. He could listen to his Sonatas and Partitas for Solo Violin over and over, in different renditions."

"He really loved stringed instruments."

"That he did. He drove his passion for strings so far as to turn his granddaughter into a violinist . . ."

Midori burst out laughing, then continued: "He sought refuge in music, like you said. No, *refuge* is maybe not the right word."

She hurried to correct herself, and after a moment of hesitation went on: "He had an extremely intense relationship with music. It was something absolutely vital to him, for mental stability . . . his mind had been left particularly vulnerable by the war. He never told me anything about his life as a soldier, what he'd been through in the army, except once. From that collective madness, which military music glorified to excess, he'd kept nothing but a nightmarish memory, I think."

Midori gave a faint smile tinged with sadness; Rei found it impossible to respond.

The violinist continued: "So he told me, once, just once . . . it was so exceptional that it stayed with me. The way he spoke—it was as if it were to someone who wasn't there, as if he were talking to himself: 'We committed atrocities. Everything we did, even the most barbaric, inhuman acts, was considered justified in the name of the emperor. Never again, anything like that, never again. I'm ashamed I survived.' After this abrupt confession, he sank into a listless state, as if he were meditating."

"It's perfectly understandable, coming from someone who had lost his entire family to the war." Then Rei began speaking in a hushed voice, one from beyond the grave, conversing with someone living inside him: "Lieutenant Kurokami survived the atomic bomb, in a manner of speaking. He belonged to the living dead, or the dead who are alive. Someone who had died once and went on living . . . or someone who was alive but lived like a dead man. Like an Auschwitz survivor . . . maybe. I'm a bit that way myself. No, I'm exaggerating. It's indecent, what I'm saying . . ."

There was a moment of silence.

". . . but the war took my entire family away from me, my father, that is . . . since my family was only him. There were just the two of us. He'd lost his parents at a very young age. He lost his wife when I was three. Apparently, my mother's parents never recovered from their daughter's untimely death. They both died of cancer, one after the other, when I was eight, then nine years old. It was a hecatomb, all around me, while I was growing up."

A leaden silence fell, much longer than the previous one.

Then, "Oh, why am I telling you all this—forgive me."

Rei reached for his cup and drank down all the remaining tea, which was cold.

"I'll put on the water," said Ayako Yamazaki, getting to her feet.

"Do you know why Mr. Kurokami was so insistent on visiting Mirecourt in addition to Cremona? Did he tell you why? The splendor of Cremona has remained intact, whereas the glory of Mirecourt has largely vanished in our time. So why bother?"

"It's true, it was a dreary little town. A bit depressing—" said Midori's mother.

"—whereas in the nineteenth century it was a prosperous

place—it seems there were as many as six hundred luthiers! Something I found out afterward . . . " added Midori.

"Yes, indeed, all downhill after that," said Rei.

"I think he simply wanted to introduce me to the major hub of French instrument making. I remember what he said a few years after that trip. That I had to see Cremona because it was the city of Stradivari, Amati, Guarneri. And as for Mirecourt, it was a necessary stop, given the importance of the Vuillaume family. He often said, 'There aren't only the Italians. In France, there's Vuillaume! Jean-Baptiste and Nicolas François!'"

5

.

AYAKO CAME BACK WITH THE TEAPOT FILLED WITH HOT WATER.
When she began pouring the tea into the three cups, Rei turned
to speak to her. "Mr. Kurokami died in . . . ?"

"In 1993," said Ayako. "Six years after our memorable trip
to Europe. A time of mourning . . . It was very difficult. In 1995,
my husband died of a heart attack."

"Were your father's last years peaceful?"

"He spent the last three years of his life in a facility
equipped for his physical and mental state. Not long after the
trip to Europe he was diagnosed with senile dementia. In the
beginning we managed at home. But after a while it just became too difficult. He had trouble walking. We had to watch
him constantly so he wouldn't fall or do something stupid.
Midori was frequently absent because of her studies: she went
to the Conservatoire every day, even when she didn't have any
classes. As for me, I was working part-time, and I couldn't
be home all the time. So, we opted for the retirement home
solution, even though it was not what I wanted."

"But, Mama, that was *the* solution! Grandfather was very
happy there, I'm sure of it. Since we visited often and saw him
regularly, he thought he was at home!"

"Not always. I'd say, rather, that he didn't know where he

was. His memory, his sense of time and place, was profoundly detached. He forgot even the most recent events. He couldn't remember his caregivers' names, or the other residents'. He asked me for news of his parents who'd died in Hiroshima. He fretted when he thought his wife, who had died years before, had not come home yet. Different eras were all mixed up in his head. It was hard to follow his logic. I accepted everything he did or said. I didn't contradict him. It was pointless to do so."

Midori listened while her mother gave these details of her grandfather's life, some of which she was hearing for the first time. When her mother fell silent, she began to speak. "His difficulties with memory and reason were sometimes so great that I couldn't keep up the conversation. Do you remember, Mama, from time to time he became completely delirious? More and more often, actually, toward the end. And then you couldn't understand a thing he was saying. All you could do was say, 'Yes, yes,' nothing more."

"Yes, there were times he would spend the entire day saying, 'There was nothing I could do, there was nothing I could do.'"

"And he said, 'What became of my boy?' when he only ever had a daughter, my mother. When he was confused like that, the only thing we could do was listen to music together. After several attempts I eventually understood that it was Bach's Sonatas and Partitas for Solo Violin, more than anything, and Schubert's quartets, that managed to give him some peace . . ."

"It's true, it was like magic! I followed Midori's advice and often put on those CDs when I went to see him. And every time, he would say, 'Ah, I've been wanting to hear this for ages!' even if it was music he'd heard just the day before."

As he listened, eyes lowered, to the young violinist and her mother describing the final, tormented phase of Lieutenant Kurokami's life, Rei tried to imagine the mental and emotional state of the former army officer and Hiroshima survivor in those very moments, in his room at the retirement home, when he listened to that music for strings, with its singularly soothing properties. Rei sat motionless for a long while, like a monk trying to create a void in his heart. Midori became concerned. "Is everything all right, Mr. Mizusawa?"

Midori and Ayako exchanged glances. "Are you all right, Mr. Mizusawa?"

"Yes, yes . . . Forgive me, I was miles away. You know, that Sunday, before they were stopped by the soldiers, my father and his Chinese friends were rehearsing Schubert's *Rosamunde*. I don't remember whether I mentioned that in my letter . . ."

"No, you didn't mention it. Well, at least I don't think you gave me that detail."

"I knew it was a string quartet, but I didn't know exactly which work they were rehearsing. It was Philippe, my French adoptive father, who subsequently told me that it was Schubert's *Rosamunde*. He had stopped by, that day, to visit with my father. But because of the rehearsal, in fact, they couldn't talk. So they agreed to meet that evening. Philippe didn't stay long. He nevertheless had the time to listen to the very beginning of *Rosamunde*. He heard, maybe not the entire first movement, but a good portion of the Allegro ma non troppo. He always told me he'd preserved a vivid memory of the emotion he felt at the time. So you see, that's how I know the piece they were working on was *Rosamunde*."

"It's a sublime work," said Midori, her voice full of wonder.

"There's another piece my father played . . . solo, after the soldiers arrived. I was in the wardrobe. I was trembling. But I dared look through the keyhole a few times . . . The soldiers stood there, motionless, opposite a superior officer who was tall and slender, it must have been your grandfather . . . My father's violin was on the floor, ruined . . . It had been trampled on."

"How awful! You cannot imagine how upset I was, when I read that your father's violin had been crushed under a soldier's feet. It's unthinkable!"

"Yes, it's terrible. But men are capable of killing other men. So it's little surprise that they are also capable of destroying a violin . . . a simple violin. It's conceivable . . ."

"I'm sure that for your father, the violin was a part of him, of his own body."

"To be sure . . . yes, absolutely. In short, at one point, some-one asked my father to play something else. It must have been Mr. Kurokami, I don't see who else it could have been. So he played a piece, a very short piece . . . probably with the Chinese violinist's instrument, since his was now useless. It lasted only three or four minutes. What could it have been? I had no way of knowing. Who else heard the music, besides me? Your father . . . who is no longer on this earth; the soldiers, who cannot be found and who in all likelihood are no longer alive; finally, the three Chinese musicians, whom I never saw again . . . So there are no witnesses. I had no idea what that short piece could have been . . . until one day I had a flash of recognition while listening to the Gavotte en rondeau from Bach's Third Partita for Solo Violin."

Rei broke off abruptly. A wave of emotion rose in his chest, obliging him to pause for a moment and catch his breath.

"How extraordinary, Bach's music has caused the entire weight of time to melt away," exclaimed Midori.

In response, Rei looked up at the ceiling and spread his arms.

"It was in 1972 or 1973," he continued, "not long after I moved to Paris. You know, during my training as a luthier, I listened to a great number of recordings of music for the violin. In the beginning they weren't great—the old 78 rpm records— but when the era of the LP came along, I tried to familiarize myself with the particular sound of every great performer. One day I was listening to a recording of Menuhin playing the Sonatas and Partitas for Solo Violin. And when the Gavotte en rondeau came on, something strange happened: it seemed to me that I could hear my father's violin in the contours of Menuhin's phrasing. The distance of over thirty years was suddenly erased, as if my father were playing there in front of me . . . I think that that day, just before he was taken to the military police station, he played the Gavotte en rondeau, maybe at Lieutenant Kurokami's request."

All at once, without a word of explanation, Midori asked Rei to come into the music room.

Rei sank into one of the two armchairs. Ayako sat on the sofa across from him. The violinist went over to the grand piano where her violin lay. She removed it from its case and spent a few seconds tuning. Then she began to play the Gavotte en rondeau. The orange light of late afternoon slanted into the music room through the large window overlooking the garden. It lit the lower half of her slim body as she swayed gently to the rhythm of the clear music flowing from her Stradivarius.

6
.

AFTER SHE HAD PUT HER VIOLIN BACK IN ITS CASE, MIDORI SAT down next to her mother and turned to Rei. "As I told you, my grandfather often listened to Bach's Sonatas and Partitas. I myself played the Gavotte en rondeau for him on several occasions, at his request."

"At his request?!"

"Yes, at his request. I can't tell you how many times exactly, but I definitely played this little treasure for him more than once. That could be yet another piece of evidence for your case."

"Yes, totally."

"And what is astonishing is that he, too, loved Menuhin's version above all others."

"Really? That's incredible, incredible . . ."

Rei paused again, lost in emotion.

7
.

"MR. MIZUSAWA, IF I READ YOUR LETTER CORRECTLY, YOU
initially began your apprenticeship in Mirecourt. Then you
went to Cremona and stayed there a long time, longer than
in Mirecourt."

"Yes. I stayed in Mirecourt for five years, and sixteen in
Cremona. A lot of French luthiers learn their profession in
Mirecourt, but in my case, I had to go and study in Cremona,
too. Because the most important thing, I would say the only
thing, my only goal in life, from the moment I dedicated myself to the art of instrument making, was to repair or restore
my father's ruined violin. To do that, I had to learn all the
necessary techniques from a master particularly skilled in
restoring stringed instruments."

"So you restored your father's violin?" asked Ayako.

"Yes."

"That's amazing!"

"It took a long, long time, because until I was sufficiently
sure of myself, I couldn't get started . . . My father's violin was
severely damaged. My master even told me it wasn't worth it.
But I absolutely had to save it. It was all I had left of my father. It was really in terrible condition. A barbaric soldier had
stomped on it with all his weight. It was broken . . . into tiny
pieces . . . down to its very soul, its soul post."

"Good Lord!" exclaimed Midori. "Even the soul post was fractured! So the soundboard was splintered?"

"Oh, yes. Not only the soundboard, but also the neck, the fingerboard, the ribs, the bridge, everything, practically everything had to be rebuilt. The back, too, was damaged, but less so. The only parts left intact were the scroll and the pegs."

"You can hardly speak of restoration anymore. You virtually had to rebuild it from scratch," Midori said.

"In a way, yes. But I wanted to save everything that *could be saved*. That's why I planned to proceed slowly, very slowly, step by step, piece by piece, point by point. I wanted every procedure, every stage involved in repairing a part of the instrument to be perfect, flawless. For me the aim was to take my father's violin back to its initial state, to restore it to the health it had always known, as if through some sort of radical surgery I were mending my father's entire wounded body . . ."

Rei shuddered with the silent twisting of emotion inside him, and for the third time he could not speak.

The two women remained silent, no longer daring to ask him any questions. All they could hear was his breathing, which in the space of a few seconds had become noticeably louder, markedly more accelerated than usual. They exchanged a glance. Then Midori stood up and went over to the shelves filled with sheet music. She reached for a large volume that was being used as a bookend. She came back and sat next to her mother, opening the book to a page with several photographs, one of them quite yellowed. She placed the open album down in front of Rei. Withdrawn into a prolonged silence, he was breathing like an asthmatic.

8
.

THE SILENCE YAWNED LIKE A DARK, DEEP CAVERN. IT LED TO the murky past, to a smooth, tranquil flow of living images and imperishable memories. Rei immersed himself in his entire career as a luthier. How he had arrived in the town of Jean-Baptiste Vuillaume and begun his apprenticeship with Maître Laberte. His meeting with Hélène, his training in Cremona with the renowned master luthier and restorer Lorenzo Zapatini. The beginning, finally, of his *life work*, as he sometimes called it, at the age of forty-three, thirty-two years after the event, after the catastrophic event that had fractured his father's soul in the same act of savage destruction inflicted on his violin, to the very annihilation of the instrument's soul post. Hard labor, requiring the patience of a bonze. Maestro Zapatini's kindness, as he oversaw Rei's work, down to the tiniest detail, with an almost paternal attentiveness. All because he knew why his disciple was putting so much effort and determination into restoring a singularly damaged violin, a violin that, moreover, was not as valuable as a genuine instrument of an old master. Rei recalled what his master had said, after painstakingly following his work for an entire year: "Now you can stand on your own two feet. Go on. But if you need advice, you can always come to me."

And so Rei had decided to return to Paris and set up on

his own. It was in 1971. Hélène, whom he'd seen only once or twice a year, summer and winter, and with whom he'd never stopped corresponding all through his long period of exile in Cremona, had set up her own business in Paris, opening a small bow-making workshop on the rue La Boétie in the eighth arrondissement. Rei had found a tiny studio, measuring 160 square feet, not far from the place de Clichy. He had worked there, lived there—the studio served as his room, his kitchen, and his workshop—for two years, and during that time he'd seen Hélène once or twice a week, no more. It was all he could do to ensure his survival and life as a craftsman in the all-consuming vastness of the capital. He had manufactured a few violins and cellos; he had done repairs and restorations; he'd seen to the maintenance and upkeep of both old and modern instruments. He'd had only very little time, consequently, to devote to his father, but his father had never been forgotten.

Over time Rei managed to establish an outstanding reputation among instrumentalists. Serious and precise in his work; honest, always keeping to deadlines, attentive to both the instrument and the artist, he had steadily expanded his clientele, ranging from soloists and orchestra musicians to high-level amateurs, by way of students at the Conservatoire. In six or seven years, he moved from 160 to 350 square feet, then to 500 and, suddenly, nearly 1,000. Moreover, through a stroke of luck, on the rue de Naples he found the perfect location for his workshop, not far from the Conservatoire on the rue de Madrid. From then on, he could devote more time to his father. A few years after his return to Paris he had finally found the necessary peace in his soul for the work of repairing and restoring his father's violin.

So a long period was spent in the solitude of his workshop, confronted by his father's mutilated instrument; but slowly, very slowly, it reclaimed the face it had first worn, and the brilliance of its health was regained.

9.

"THANK YOU FOR SHOWING ME THESE PHOTOGRAPHS. ON THIS one, most of all, I think I recognize the face that appeared before me that day, backlit, the face of the man who handed me the violin, the Black God . . ."

The sun was setting. Rei looked at his watch.

"It's already five o'clock! I've taken too much of your time—forgive me."

"No, not at all, Mr. Mizusawa. You've come from so far—from Paris, on the one hand, and on the other, from your past in Japan, so long ago. I didn't see the time go by. I'm so glad we could talk about my grandfather together. Today the picture I had of him has been enriched with subtle textures and nuance. I am sincerely grateful."

Rei bowed his head slightly, then hesitated for a moment, unable to express himself. Finally, he bent down to pick up the violin case he'd left next to his armchair. He opened it and took out the instrument that slept inside.

"This is my father's restored violin."

"Goodness, you brought it with you!" cried Ayako.

"There may be only 15 or 20 percent left of what my father knew, but thanks to your grandfather it survived the carnage. It was originally made by Nicolas François Vuillaume, the younger brother of Jean-Baptiste Vuillaume. I found his signature inside. I don't know whether, that day, my father had time to tell Lieutenant Kurokami that it was a violin made by the younger brother of the great Vuillaume. I don't know why, or how, this violin ended up in my father's hands."

"If Grandfather was so insistent upon going to Mirecourt, couldn't it be because he remembered your father's violin? In all likelihood he had heard from Mr. Mizusawa himself that it was a Nicolas François . . ."

"Yes, you're right, Midori," her mother agreed. "That would explain why my father got it into his head that we absolutely had to go to Mirecourt."

"What a beautiful instrument!"

"I completely rebuilt the soundboard, the ribs . . . anyway, extensively. I redid the varnish as well. So the violin's appearance changed significantly. Your grandfather wouldn't recognize it. Inside, next to Nicolas François Vuillaume's label I placed my own, in smaller characters."

"May I try it?"

"Yes, of course. I would be very honored."

Midori Yamazaki reached for the brilliant dark red violin, returned from its bloody past, a violin once murdered, then rescued, first by her grandfather Kengo Kurokami, Black God, then miraculously resurrected by the son, now a luthier, of its owner, who disappeared forever one autumn morning in the year 1938. Just as, after a few seconds of tuning, she was about to play, a thought occurred to her. She went back to Rei and asked him, pointing to the bow that was still in the case, "Would it be better if I used that bow?"

"Not necessarily. It's a bow made by Hélène, my companion,

uh, wife. She tried to create this bow with a particular thought to my father's restored violin."

"Well, then, I'll play with your wife's bow."

Midori set down her bow to take Hélène's. Standing in the very spot where she had played the Gavotte en rondeau two hours earlier, she performed the piece by Bach again. The high notes echoed like a long ripple of pure raindrops falling from a troubled, low-lying sky, sparkling with the first few rays of sunshine as it angled through the verdant foliage of a lush northern forest. The medium and bass notes were as if padded, slipping over an expanse of velvet, and giving rise to the impression of close warmth that emanates from a marble hearth where the fire is kept burning all night. There was, moreover, an astonishing evenness of timbre. The music surged forth, ebbed, rising and falling with euphoric freedom. It made one think of a gleeful, skipping dance: the joy of passing through an enchanted landscape.

10

.

"IT HAS A WONDERFUL SOUND. YOU'VE DONE A MAGNIFICENT job, Mr. Mizusawa! There is a great consistency of sound in every register, on every string . . . It's very impressive! It really makes me want to play it."

"Do you mean that? Do you really mean that?"

"Yes, yes, I really do, this instrument strikes me as exceptional. It's not every day I come across something like it."

Midori delicately returned the violin and its bow to their case on the rectangular table between the sofa and the armchairs, where the day's last rays of sunlight fell.

"Well, then, I will entrust this violin to you. I'm leaving it to you. I would be happy if you would help it blossom, grow . . . I finished the restoration work in 1982, and since then I've had the opportunity to show it to several violinists. Some of them wanted to buy it, but I always told them it was not for sale."

"I can assure you, Mr. Mizusawa, that any professional violinist would want to play it."

"Your grandfather saved it. Your grandfather wanted you to study the violin. You have become a world-renowned violinist. It's only fair that I leave it with you, if you think it can join you to produce music that is to your liking. My father's violin would be much happier in your home than in mine. It needs to use its voice."

"Oh, Mr. Mizusawa . . ."

Stunned and shaken through her entire being by the sudden, unimaginable offering, Midori was speechless. She turned to her mother, who seemed to be just as astounded, if not more so. After a long silence, Midori spoke again, holding back the tears that were about to overwhelm her: "Thank you, Mr. Mizusawa. I don't know what to say. This is a wonderful gift. I really didn't expect something like this."

She had to pause, to wait for the wave of emotion to recede.

"Thank you for placing your trust in me. I don't know how to thank you. I will take great care of your violin, of your father. I will send you news of it from time to time."

This was how it came to be, sixty-five years later, that Yu Mizusawa's violin—brought back to life by Yu Mizusawa's son, Rei-Jacques Maillard, once he had become a renowned master luthier—returned to the family of the very person who had entrusted it to the little boy seeking refuge that afternoon. He had been trying to hide, curled up in a ball in the stifling darkness of a protective wardrobe, after the violin, originally made by Nicolas François Vuillaume, had been barbarically shattered.

11

NOW THAT HE HAD ENTRUSTED HIS VIOLIN—THE VIOLIN
made by Nicolas François Vuillaume, his father's resuscitated
violin—to Midori Yamazaki, the Black God's granddaughter,
the weight of the burden Rei Mizusawa had carried all those
long, endless years was dispelled. The chain of the ball he had
dragged behind him everywhere had been broken.

The next morning, as soon as he awoke, he felt ready to
explore Tokyo. He had an entire day free before he was scheduled to fly back to Paris. His steps led him quite naturally to
the Shibuya district where he had lived over sixty-five years
earlier. In half a century Tokyo had been transformed: Rei
knew in advance that he would not find or recognize anything
there. That was why he started with a visit to the town hall in
Shibuya, to obtain a few reliable points of reference.

In the archives department the visitor explained to a fifty-
something employee that he was looking for the former site of
the municipal cultural center, as it existed back in 1938. The
clerk went to fetch a huge volume that contained some old
maps. He opened the pages corresponding to the period and
easily found the spot where it used to be.

"It has changed a great deal, you know. The city was completely razed in 1945."

"Yes, I heard over one hundred thousand people died

and a million were injured during the air raid on March 10. And that three hundred B-29 bombers filled the sky like a cloud of flies, dropping 380,000 incendiary bombs in two hours . . ."

"Yes. It must have been horrific. The kind of hell that ensued—you could almost compare it to the atomic bomb in Hiroshima, which killed as many in a few seconds. The result was the same, with the exception, of course, of radioactivity. On March 10 it was the working-class neighborhoods to the east that were targeted. Here in Shibuya, the raids in May were the worst."

"Postwar reconstruction must have changed the neighborhoods beyond recognition."

"Certainly."

Answering the old man without raising his head, the fifty-something employee alternated between the contemporary map and the map from 1935–40. He also paused for a moment on one that showed the areas destroyed by the successive firebombings of Tokyo in 1945.

"I've tried to localize the cultural center on this new map. You can get started with it. You'll see for yourself. Maybe a few small streets survived."

"Thank you, sir. You've been very kind."

"You're very welcome. Are you doing research?"

"No, I used to live here, until 1938. I've come to see the neighborhood where I grew up, after living abroad for over sixty years."

"Ah, I see!"

"I'd like to go to the place where my parents lived. The postal address included the word Shinsen, if I remember correctly. It means 'fountain of God,' doesn't it?"

"Yes. That's funny, I'd forgotten the meaning of Shinsen."

He looked again at the map of the areas that had burned in 1945. After a moment's silence, the municipal archivist said, "The Shinsen district isn't far from here. If you like, I can mark it on the map I gave you."

"Oh, thank you, that's very kind."

"There. With a bit of luck, you'll find a few traces of the place you knew. As far as I can tell from the map, this entire zone south of Shinsen station escaped destruction. Well, then, enjoy your walk around the fountain of God!"

"Thank you, sir, very much."

After walking for half an hour Rei came to a building that housed a small neighborhood public library. This was where the house of culture, as it was commonly known at the time, used to stand. What he saw prompted nothing. He continued walking. When he came to a little crossroads he noticed, on the far side of a rubble stone wall, a majestic cherry tree with black, gnarly branches. He turned down a little street where there were fewer shops, and behind him, the rumble of the city grew fainter. It was there, contrary to all expectation, that a space suddenly opened up before Rei.

His feet and legs guided him. A new sensation came over him. Once again, he picked up the movements and rhythms of his body as he had recorded them that day, heading home, accompanied by a Shiba Inu that had simply mysteriously appeared in his path.

He stopped outside a newly constructed little house. It must have been made of wood, although its beige surface imitated brickwork. He looked all around. He saw nothing that reminded him of his childhood. His particular spatial awareness told him, however, that it might have been here. Then he saw himself seated, as he had been, a small eleven-year-old boy. Night slowly falling. The light from the street lamp coming from his left. He could feel the warmth of the animal spreading to his belly. He gradually fell asleep . . .

12
.

THAT NIGHT, MOMO CAME TO SEE HIM, ALL THE WAY TO THE
bed in his hotel room.

IV

ALLEGRO MODERATO

1.

REI KNOCKED ON THE DOOR.

"Come in," said a voice in Japanese, a woman's voice, tired and feeble.

It was a private room, overlooking the hospital garden. A nurse in uniform, a stethoscope in her ears, was taking the blood pressure of an elderly woman who lay in an elevated hospital bed. The nurse turned to Rei and raised her hand to indicate that he should wait. During all this time, the old lady smiled silently at Rei.

The nurse, looping her stethoscope around her neck, jotted the patient's blood pressure on a sheet of paper and spoke a few words to Rei, which he totally failed to comprehend. The old lady then said to him, in a reedy voice: "She says you can take the chair and sit next to me."

The even, rhythmic words the old lady uttered in clear, flowing Japanese reminded the visitor of the quiver he'd felt as a schoolboy when he'd heard her clear voice expressing and articulating Japanese so naturally and fluidly. Now her voice was deeper and slightly hoarse, but she had preserved a sort of smooth cadence that caused the language to chime so wonderfully.

"Xièxiè." Rei said the only word he knew in Chinese, *thank you.*

He sat down next to the bed and took the elderly patient's emaciated right hand. Overcome with emotion, she could not keep her tears from welling. The early afternoon sunlight cast its luminous clarity onto the white comforter. In a Shanghai hospital room, the conversation resumed between two people who had met fleetingly in Tokyo over half a century earlier.

2
.

ONE DAY IN THE SPRING OF 2004 REI HAD RECEIVED AN EMAIL
from a young Chinese man who said he was contacting him
on behalf of his great-aunt Lin Yanfen. The message was in
Japanese. The author said he was writing to Rei Mizusawa for
his great-aunt, because she wished to get in touch with him,
to inquire whether he was the son of a certain Yu Mizusawa,
whom she had known in Tokyo in 1937–38.

Lin Yanfen, hospitalized for a late-stage cancer that was
destroying her liver, was aware she did not have long to live.
She had told her great-nephew of her desire to find the son
of Yu Mizusawa, who'd been arrested by the military police
one Sunday afternoon in 1938 during a rehearsal of the string
quartet they had formed with two other Chinese musicians.
The great-nephew was eager to please his great-aunt, so he began searching for Rei Mizusawa on the internet. He had found
several people with the same name and had taken note of their
professional trajectory; he then conveyed to his great-aunt the
fruits of his labor. When Lin Yanfen came upon several decisive clues—"orphan," "French adoptive father," "trained as a
luthier in France and Italy," and so on—featured on the personal
website of one Rei Mizusawa, Master Luthier, she told herself
that this was likely the person she hoped to contact. And so,

she dictated a short letter in Japanese to her great-nephew, for him to send via email.

From: Yu Jian
To: Rei Mizusawa / Jacques Maillard
Subject: On behalf of Lin Yanfen
Date: April 29, 2004

Hello. My name is Yu Jian. I'm writing to you on behalf of my great-aunt Lin Yanfen, whom you must certainly remember. This is a letter she has written to you from her hospital bed in Shanghai:

I was in Tokyo as an agronomy student from 1934 to 1938. I met your father, Yu Mizusawa, who invited me and two other Chinese friends to play in a string quartet. My memories of that time are unforgettable. In 1938, one Sunday afternoon, we were rehearsing a Schubert quartet in a room at the house of culture in Shibuya when a group of soldiers burst in and violently ordered us to stop. Your father, who had sensed danger when he heard the sound of boots approaching, hid you inside a wardrobe just in time. That day, during our rehearsal, you had been immersed in your reading; I didn't catch the name of the book. But, if you are Yu Mizusawa's son, you must remember.

If these few lines you have just read mean anything to you, I would be very happy to receive a quick reply.

Looking forward to hearing from you,
Lin Yanfen

Rei replied at once to the Chinese woman's message, confirming that he was indeed the boy lost in his reading—a book titled *How Do You Live?*—during the rehearsal of his father's quartet. Three days later, a second letter arrived via email from Lin Yanfen.

From: Yu Jian
To: Rei Mizusawa / Jacques Maillard
Subject: I am so happy . . .
Date: May 2, 2004

Dear Rei,

I am so happy to know we can be in touch now, you cannot imagine! I bless the internet!

I am ninety-two years old, and am spending my last days in a hospital in Shanghai. I am indeed very ill; I surely have only a few months to live.

The reason I wrote you, with the help of my great-nephew, who studied Japanese in university and, on top of that, is a computer expert, is because I'd like to see you again, in order to return two mementos that were your father's. Since I am ill, I can't come to you. Do you think it would be possible for you to come and visit me in Shanghai? If you don't think that's a possibility, I will send these two items to you by mail.

I eagerly await your reply,
Lin Yanfen

Rei hurriedly booked a flight to Shanghai and a hotel room. He then replied to Lin Yanfen to inform her he would be leaving for China in a week's time.

3.

REI TOLD THE ELDERLY CHINESE LADY HOW HE HAD MANAGED that Sunday, until nightfall, after his father and his musician friends had vanished: the episode with Lieutenant Kurokami gingerly handing him the ruined violin, his strange encounter with the Shiba Inu on the way home, and the arrival of his father's French friend, Philippe, who found him asleep out-side the house, protected by the warmth of the dog that had curled up between Rei's chest and his legs, tucking itself under him . . .

Yanfen, lying in her bed, which was once again horizontal, asked Rei if it was the French reporter who had helped him.

"Yes, I couldn't get in the house that day since I didn't have the key. I told Philippe what had happened after he left. We waited for a while in darkness, then Philippe decided it would be best to take me to his house instead of waiting for my father's increasingly unlikely return. Philippe kept me at his place for a while. I think he did everything he possibly could to find out what became of my father."

"So he must have told you that your father was taken to the military police."

"Yes . . . but I think he told me very little about what he might have found out . . ."

"That's normal. You were too young. How old were you?"

"Eleven."

"He wanted to protect you from too great a shock."

"When he understood that my father would never be coming back, he decided to adopt me. He knew I was an orphan, completely alone in the world. In the context of the war, which had turned Japan into an uncontrollable monster, Philippe and his wife decided to return to France a few weeks after that tragic Sunday."

"He did right. Ah, if only Yu had known . . ."

"Yes, he must have been sick with worry about what might happen to me."

The old woman in bed wiped tears from her cheeks with a white cotton handkerchief. The French visitor waited a bit longer before picking up the thread of their conversation.

"In any case, that is why I grew up in France as Philippe and Isabelle Maillard's adoptive son."

Rei shared a few memories of his French childhood.

Yanfen nodded from time to time as she listened to Rei, who was still holding her hand in his. From time to time she breathed heavily, as if she were afraid of suffocating.

Rei stopped speaking.

A long, deep silence enfolded the sick old lady and the old man. He had come from so far away for this intense communion; both of them were deeply troubled and moved by the way their respective paths in life had crossed so unexpectedly.

"And so you became a luthier."

"Yes. After a few false starts, I turned rather quickly to making instruments. I wanted to restore my father's violin. I'd always kept it with me, in its half-dead state, like a corpse decomposing. I apprenticed initially in Mirecourt, then in Cremona. Making instruments became my only passion."

Lin Yanfen closed her eyes and hid her face with her left hand.

There was a knock at the door. A doctor in his fifties entered, accompanied by a nurse (not the one who'd taken Yanfen's blood pressure). The doctor greeted Rei with a slight bow, then went up to Yanfen and took her left hand to check her pulse. He spoke cheerily to his patient, his voice lively and resonant, while she replied in a frail, faint voice. Rei didn't understand what they were saying, but he could sense in the doctor's good-natured attitude a tactful attention and desire to be there for his dying patient. He took Yanfen's small hand in his large ones, nodded to the visitor, and left the room, dictating a few words to the nurse, who jotted them down like a stenographer at full speed on a clipboard dangling from her neck. Rei asked the nurse in a hushed voice in English, "Excuse me, can I still stay here? I wouldn't disturb her."

"Yes. You can stay," she replied, in French. "Quite the opposite, it does her good to have you here to talk to her! That's what we think. She has told us some of her story . . . and yours, too." The woman in white had whispered all this in a French that flowed quite naturally, with the trace of an affable smile.

The foreign visitor was surprised by her sudden use of French.

"You speak very good French!"

"I studied it at university, then went for a year on a training course in France . . . in Toulouse. I have such good memories of my time there."

"That's wonderful."

"If you have any concerns, you can find me in the treatment room."

Rei barely had time to say a simple "thanks" before she vanished into the corridor. He turned back to the bed. Yanfen seemed to be sleeping. Rei left the room on tiptoe, resolved to return in half an hour's time.

4

YANFEN WAS STILL SLEEPING WHEN REI CAUTIOUSLY OPENED
the door. He sat on the chair next to the bed, not making a
sound. He looked at the old lady lying in bed. He examined
her face furrowed with wrinkles, her half-open mouth, her
pale, hollow cheeks. He remembered the emotion that had
come over him, that Sunday, on seeing her face, radiant with
beauty, and her slender, fragile body. That was the first time,
he thought, he'd felt an obscure force welling inside him to
trouble his heart.

"Forgive me, I fell asleep."

"Don't apologize, I was glad to see you sleeping so peacefully."

Yanfen looked at the alarm clock on the bedside table.

"I didn't sleep for long . . ."

"No, just over half an hour."

"I'm not supposed to sleep during the day. It keeps me from
sleeping normally. But, in fact, I haven't slept well in a very
long time."

"No?"

"Rei, I have to tell you what happened after you were separated from your father for good."

"Yes, if it's not too tiring for you."

"No, it won't tire me. On the contrary, I'm glad to be able to talk with you. You were kind enough to make the journey. I owe you the story of what you don't know. And above all I must give you the things in the cloth bag placed there in the cupboard."

Yanfen asked Yu Mizusawa's son to retrieve the bag from the cupboard and open it.

"Inside, there's a book and a cardigan."

"A book and a cardigan?"

"Yes. But first of all, I must tell you what happened after the scene you witnessed from the wardrobe—"

"After the music by Bach my father played—"

"Yes. The Gavotte en rondeau he performed so magnificently. We were all amazed, filled with emotion—including, I think, the soldier who had asked him to play."

"So it was the Gavotte en rondeau after all."

"Yes. I remember it as if it were yesterday."

Yanfen was staring into space. Not saying a word, Rei placed his right hand on the sick woman's shriveled hand, where it lay on top of the comforter like a dead leaf the wind had forgotten to blow away. It was cold.

"The soldiers took us to a detention center. After twenty-four hours, our two Chinese friends, Kang and Cheng, were released . . . probably thanks to their status as scholarship students. But not your father or me. I think there is one detail that you probably weren't aware of. The soldiers thought I was your father's wife."

"Really? Why is that?"

"When they were asking each of us for our identity, your father declared that I was his wife and that my name was Aiko. He wanted to protect me . . . I suppose."

"No, you're right, I didn't know that."

"Back then, the Chinese were viewed with suspicion, even scorn."

"I wonder if it isn't still like that. What became of your two Chinese friends, by the way? Did you stay in touch?"

"No, I lost sight of them. When they finally allowed me to leave, I went right away to get my viola from the storage room in the cultural center. Their instruments were gone. As was Yu's broken violin, for that matter. I was a little afraid—I even dared to open the wardrobe, you know . . . but you weren't there anymore, of course. It was both reassuring and worrying. 'Where is he? What has become of him?'"

Lin Yanfen looked up and sighed, as if she were silently protesting the decisions of heaven.

"It could be that Cheng, the cellist, stayed in Japan to live with his Japanese wife. As for Kang, the second violin, I never had any news."

"So after a while they released you?"

"Yes. I spent two days and two nights in the prison. They kept me longer, no doubt, because I obstinately went on playing the role of spouse."

"They subjected you to a formal interrogation?"

"Two probing interrogations, yes. But I was released forty-eight hours later."

"Were you with my father, in the same—"

"No, they separated us. I couldn't see him. After I got out,

I went back to the military police every day to ask to see your father, making the most of my title as spouse. But initially they wouldn't allow me to see him, under the pretext that he'd been detained for reasons to do with the Public Security Preservation Law."

"Ah, that fiendish law—so many people were imprisoned, tortured, and killed in its name."

"Yes, that's it. Only after four or five days had gone by was I able to see him. He'd clearly been beaten, mistreated, abused, tortured. He looked thinner, gaunt with fatigue. He was like a ghost. I remember, he said . . ."

Choking with emotion, Yanfen could not speak. She waited a few seconds, then went on, tears in her throat: "He told me that the soldiers from the military police had searched his house and found 'lots of dangerous books' and that they were accusing him of 'being contaminated by communist ideas and contaminating others with the same ideas.' We were only allowed to speak for twenty minutes. It went by in the blink of an eye. Naturally the only thing he cared about was you. He wondered what had happened to you. He imagined all sorts of possible scenarios. It was the cruelest torment for him. And I couldn't tell him anything, unfortunately."

"That was another torture he had to endure . . . not knowing what had happened to me . . ."

"Exactly."

Rei lowered his head. Then he took it in both hands as if forcing himself to put up with an acute pain in his gut. A dark silence spread. Until he heard the old woman's hoarse voice murmur: "In the end, your father even had the kindness to advise me to go back to China as soon as possible: 'It would be better for you, after all, more reassuring in any case,' he said. His face was haggard, ravaged with sadness and pain. I cannot forget . . . I've never forgotten."

"After that meeting, did you manage to see him again?"

"No, that was the first and last time."

"So after that, no one ever saw him again," said the old man in a subdued voice, looking up.

"I went back to the prison. But it wasn't possible to see him. Every time, they refused. One day I ran into the man who had asked Yu, that day of the rehearsal, to prove he really was a musician in order to dispel the other soldiers' suspicions. He wasn't like the others, that one. He was amiable and courteous for a military man . . . He implied to me that from then on I would have to give up on seeing my husband again . . . 'He's gone far away—he won't be coming back,' he asserted, lowering his head. He was sorry to have to tell me so suddenly and bluntly. At that moment I thought I could see his face contract nervously, from his chin to his brow."

Rei told Yanfen about his trip to see Midori Yamazaki the previous year. Yanfen was stunned by the improbable encounter between *little* Rei, now a luthier, and the lieutenant's granddaughter, now a violinist. Once she had recovered from her initial shock, she was all ears, eager to hear about the day Rei had spent with Midori and her mother. In the end, letting out a deep sigh, she murmured: "So he, too, suffered. He didn't belong there, in the army . . ."

There was a knock at the door. The French-speaking nurse came in with two other women in white uniforms. She murmured into Rei's ear: "We've come to give her her bath—do you mind going out for a moment? We need a quarter of an hour."

"Not at all."

The nurse gave him a quick smile.

Rei left the room after telling Yanfen he'd be absent for a few minutes.

"You'll come back, won't you, because we haven't finished . . ."

"Yes, of course I will, of course."

5
.

"THE VIOLIN WAS COMPLETELY CRUSHED. THE DESPICABLE soldier destroyed it with two stamps of his boot. And you nevertheless managed to restore it?"

"Yes. It took a very long time. But I managed."

"How long did it take you?"

"I set off on that reckless undertaking the last year of my time in Cremona, under my master's watchful eye. So it was in . . . 1970. And I finished the complete restoration by 1982. So, it took me twelve years. I remember this very well, because that was the year I began to live with my bow-making friend."

"Ah, your wife is a bow maker?"

"Yes. We're not married, but it's as if we were. I met her very early on, in Mirecourt, at the beginning of my apprenticeship. Mirecourt is a tiny town, but it's been renowned for instrument making since the eighteenth century, like Cremona in Italy . . . We decided we would live together once the restoration of my father's violin was completely finished. I was fifty-five years old."

"And your wife . . . uh, partner . . . or your friend—I don't know how to put it, I don't know the right word in Japanese—"

"She's five years younger than me. Her name is Hélène. That way you know everything now!"

Lin Yanfen smiled at him for the first time.

"I'm glad to know you have someone with you. It's not an easy path, life . . . It's better to go along that path with someone, than to be on one's own, as I was."

Rei saw that Yanfen had become pensive all of a sudden, and he said, "And you, are you—"

"I stayed on my own."

There was a moment of silence. Yanfen seemed absent, lost in thought. Rei could only imagine what might be luring the old lady into her silent daydreaming.

"Would you take the cardigan and the book out of the bag?"

The cardigan, a pale pink, was carefully folded inside a transparent plastic bag, as if it were a brand new item on a shelf in a shop. The book had a protective wrapping of brown paper, so the title was hidden.

"The pink cardigan belonged to your mother, who died when you were very little."

"I think I was three—"

"One day when we were rehearsing at your place, in your house—because in the beginning that's where we rehearsed, but since there wasn't much space, later on we decided to go to the house of culture. Anyway, I was cold, I sneezed . . . and that's when your father kindly lent me this cardigan that had been your mother's. Once the rehearsal was over, I went to give it back to him before I left. And he said, 'Keep it, it's cold. You'll give it back when you feel like it. You do understand I don't need it anymore . . .' In the end, I kept it and wore it from time to time, even in front of him. I'm sorry I took advantage of his kindness—"

"No, I don't think you did. On the contrary, he must have been happy to see you wearing the cardigan. I'm sure of it."

Rei thought he saw Yanfen's pale face turn slightly pink.

"And the book?" asked Rei, picking it up.

"When we were arrested, they took us straight to the detention center. Yu had this little book in the inside pocket of his jacket. When we got there, he seized the very moment when the soldiers had dispersed to hand it to me without them seeing. And I kept it under my skirt, in my panties, to be exact, the whole time I was in custody. So they never found it. What a fright!"

Rei opened the little book. The title page appeared: *The Crab Cannery Ship*. It was a famous novel by Takiji Kobayashi, published in 1929, describing the living conditions of virtual slavery the workers endured on board a crab fishing ship in the Sea of Okhotsk, between Japan and Russia. Rei hadn't read it, but he'd heard of Takiji Kobayashi, a well-known author of proletarian literature, who died in 1933 at twenty-nine, following a brutal police interrogation—a horrendous torture session.

"I've never read this novel, even though it's famous."

"I've read it so often I've lost count. I wonder if your father didn't meet the same fate as Takiji Kobayashi."

Yanfen let out a deep sigh and lapsed into a contemplative silence.

6

.

"YOUR FATHER LOVED TO READ. AND SOME OF THE BOOKS IN HIS library proved fatal . . ."

"You both lived through that dark period. When all freedom was suppressed—freedom of thought, freedom of speech, of conscience—"

"You loved to read, too. I remember how, that day, you were immersed in a book. No one could take it away from you."

"Ah, yes, you remember?"

"Yes, I can still picture it vividly."

"It was a book by Genzaburo Yoshino, titled *How Do You Live?*, published in 1937, so a year before the tragedy. My father gave it to me. He'd read it as soon as it was available and he'd been astounded. In any case, he was very enthusiastic about it. It's a book I carried with me all through adolescence. I've kept the original copy and I reread it regularly. Do you know the book?"

"No. When I found out that Yu wouldn't be coming back, I decided to leave Japan. From then on, I was cut off from the country."

"It's a magnificent book. Right in the midst of fascist madness and infatuation with all things military and jingoistic, Yoshino was bold enough to write, for a young Japanese audience, a book that advocated the critical use of reason and defended the moral superiority of friendship among equals over the blind submission to one's elders and leaders that was rampant. I think my father wanted to raise me as a young man who could keep his wits about him in any situation, who wouldn't succumb to collective folly, and would rebel against absurdity."

On the afternoon of November 6, 1938—abruptly, without the slightest warning, without the slightest possibility of preparing himself psychologically—Rei Mizusawa had lost his father forever, but he had never stopped thinking about the man who was absent, vanished, missing, dead. He thought about him above all because of the violin reduced to smithereens, but also because of Yoshino's book. And now, thanks to the unwavering patience and loyalty of this Chinese friend, he could add the pink cardigan and *The Crab Cannery Ship* to the violin and book. Rei had made the broken violin the purpose and substance of his life. When he'd finished restoring Nicolas François Vuillaume's creation, the idea of translating Yoshino's great novel someday had occurred to him quite naturally. He thought he could hear his father's voice in the pages of *How Do You Live?*, mingling with the author's. He'd begun the translation ten or so years before. He got up early, at around five o'clock, in the silence of dawn. After a quick breakfast of coffee and a slice of buttered bread, he went to his workbench, surrounded by tools, wood shavings, and a number of instruments being crafted. He would try to relate, in French, the intellectual awakening and inner evolution of a Japanese schoolboy, as admirably depicted through Yoshino's words. He was in no hurry. He took it one step at a time, translating barely ten lines a day, word by word, sentence by sentence, paragraph by paragraph. At eleven o'clock he stopped for a break, then put his navy-blue luthier's apron back on.

"I'm doing this translation for myself alone, with no intention of publishing it. As I linger on the details of every page, I think I can hear my father's voice more clearly."

7.

THE SUN WAS SETTING. TWO TREES VISIBLE FROM THE WINDOW in the room, a cherry and a maple, roughly twenty yards apart, gradually began to slip under the darkening veil of night.

"It's getting late, Mrs. Lin. I have tired you long enough, all afternoon. It's time for me to say goodbye."

"Thank you so much for coming to me. I am so happy to have seen you again, to have heard you talk about your life, your career as a luthier, and I'm so glad I was able to give back to you what I had to return. Yu's disappearance has been, for me, a wound that never healed, but he is the one, at the same time, who helped me live. Today I'm happy because I found you. To see you before me again has truly brought me peace, an unexpected balm. Thank you, thank you so much. I can never thank you enough."

"Let us stay in touch. I can always write to your great-nephew with my news."

"Of course. That would make me very happy—you've no idea how happy that would make me."

Rei took her right hand again: it was cold, trembling slightly between his robust craftsman's hands. It was without strength.

"How warm your hands are!" Yanfen stammered.

The very old lady and the old man stayed for a long time like that, looking at each other. Then Rei lowered his head, while

Yanfen turned hers toward the window; soon, a nurse would come and draw the curtains. A few seconds later they looked at each other again. Finally, they said goodbye. The old man turned back to the very old lady before he opened the door to leave. He began to close it behind him slowly, very slowly. The patient's purple lips were tensed, but her pale face flashed the visitor one last smile. The luthier raised his left hand, timidly, in response to Yanfen's right hand, which was swinging limply, like the heavy pendulum of an old clock.

Rei walked down the dimly lit corridor toward the hospital exit. On his back he carried a small bag that contained, among other things, his mother's pink cardigan, which Yanfen had kept and worn for more than half a century, and a very old copy of *The Crab Cannery Ship* by Takiji Kobayashi that had belonged to his father, then was kept, read, and reread by their Chinese friend—his father's impromptu bride: ephemeral, fictitious, imaginary, dreamed.

8.

BACK IN PARIS, REI HURRIED TO WRITE MIDORI YAMAZAKI AND tell her of his unexpected encounter with Lin Yanfen. He wanted to share with her everything they had not known before concerning the tragedy of November 6, 1938, the part that concerned his father's fate after his arrest.

From: 水澤礼 / Rei Mizusawa / Jacques Maillard
To: Midori Yamazaki
Subject: Meeting with Lin Yanfen
Date: May 17, 2004

Dear Midori-san,

I hope you are well.

You'll find enclosed a Word file I wrote to you after my totally unexpected meeting with Lin Yanfen, the viola player from the quartet playing *Rosamunde* on November 6, 1938.

I've written you a long description, but it doesn't mean you have to reply to me. I just wanted to combine my story and that of Nicolas François Vuillaume's violin, which you now know, with the story of my father as told to me by Lin Yanfen.

Hoping all goes well for you,

With warmest regards,

水澤礼 / Rei Mizusawa / Jacques Maillard

9.

MONTHS WENT BY IN THE WORKSHOP, WHOSE WARM, COZY silence was often enhanced by muted chamber music. On a rainy November day, Rei was doing maintenance work on a Jean-Baptiste Vuillaume violin entrusted to him by a renowned American violinist. It had once, she told him, belonged to the Czech violinist Josef Suk. From the two speakers that hung from the ceiling came the quiet strains of the second movement of Schubert's *Rosamunde* quartet. Rei straightened the bridge, which was imperceptibly bent forward. He adjusted it so that it would be fixed exactly between the f-holes. Finally, handling the sound post setter with great caution, he moved the violin's sound post a few tenths of a millimeter. This was all necessary for the vibrations of the strings to be transmitted unimpeded to the bridge, and from the bridge to the sound post, from the sound post to the bass bar, and finally to reverberate throughout the instrument's entire sound box.

He took one of the perfectly aligned bows from the top drawer of an old dresser standing underneath the row of violins and violas.

Just then he heard a faint ping, indicating he'd received an electronic message. He played the first bars of the Gavotte en rondeau on the Vuillaume. Then with a satisfied expression, he placed the instrument on the big table that divided the workshop from the little sitting area.

He went to his computer, at the far end of the workbench, and opened his email inbox. There was a message from Midori Yamazaki.

From: Midori Yamazaki
To: 水澤礼 / Rei Mizusawa / Jacques Maillard
Subject: Concert in Paris
Date: November 19, 2004

Dear Mizusawa-san,

Forgive me for not getting in touch for so long. Since we met back in May 2003, a year and a half has gone by! Time seems to be passing at an incredible speed.

I went on several tours, all over the world, last year. The last was in December to Eastern Europe. At the beginning of this year, probably because I'd been overextending myself for months, I fell ill. So, in keeping with my doctor's advice, I've taken six months off to rest. Only since September have I gradually started to get back to my usual pace. Now I'm completely recovered.

I wanted to thank you for the letter you sent me following your meeting with Lin Yanfen. Now, with the missing piece, you are able to construct the full picture of what happened on November 6, 1938. And I'm happy to share this complete picture with you, where my grandfather briefly appears once again.

I'm writing to you today to let you know that I'll be in Paris next spring and I'll be giving a concert at the Salle Pleyel. I hope you'll come with your wife. You'll receive an official invitation through my agent. I'd be

delighted to see you again on this occasion. My mother will almost
certainly be there, too.

In sincere friendship,

Midori Yamazaki

Rei replied immediately to Midori to thank her for her
message and the invitation to her concert in Paris. He assured
her he would not fail to come with his wife. He could already
picture the Salle Pleyel. How could he and Hélène decline? It
was with great joy that he'd introduce her to Midori Yamazaki!
And then, after the concert, if her schedule allowed it, he'd be
very happy to see her again with her mother.

He called Hélène to tell her of the invitation he'd received
from Midori Yamazaki. She exclaimed, "What a singular des-
tiny you've had! If only it were possible to invite your father
and Lieutenant Kurokami to the concert as well!"

10
.

FEELING RATHER NERVOUS, REI AND HÉLÈNE ARRIVED AT THE
Salle Pleyel far too early. There were not many people in the
foyer yet. A handful of figures seemed to move vaguely about,
as if through the haze of a sweltering summer day. A shadowy
form materialized.

"Jacques! Hello."

"What a surprise! How are you?"

"Fine, thanks, and you? I was just thinking I might see you
here tonight. Apparently, she's a magnificent violinist. Have
you ever heard her play?"

"Yes. Well, a little. Not more than that."

"And incidentally, rumor has it that she's playing one of
your violins—is that true?"

"Who told you that? No, it can only be a rumor. Forgive me,
I've got to go, I've seen someone over there I must say hello to."

"No problem! Well, goodbye then! See you soon."

Annoyed, Rei let out a sigh, once he'd dismissed his impor-
tunate, invasive colleague. He took Hélène by the arm to go and
hide behind a column. What a nuisance that man is! You'd think
he lives off rumors, thought Rei, even more bothered. Gradually
the foyer began to fill with black jackets, dresses of various
colors, and even a few casual outfits. Hélène heard a man's
voice behind her shouting, "Program! Get your program!"

She went and bought one. As stated in the official invitation letter, Midori Yamazaki would be playing Alban Berg's concerto, *To the Memory of an Angel*. The luthier remembered the day he'd spent in the company of Midori and her mother in their house in Tokyo. He thought about Lieutenant Kurokami, Black God. He also thought about his father. Time had flown, engulfing everything in its path, forever. But the lieutenant had left his shadow among the living, just as Yu Mizusawa had.

The spectators streamed in through the doors. Rei and Hélène went to find their seats in the middle of the orchestra section, with its optimal acoustics, roughly sixty feet from the stage.

11
.

CONTRARY TO WHAT WAS USUAL FOR THE TIMES, THE CONCERT
began with Beethoven's Seventh Symphony, so that Berg's
concerto would be given the place of honor. Rei liked this
symphony very much, particularly the historic rendition con-
ducted by Furtwängler in 1943: a wild energy ran through it
from one end to the other, a lust for life, even in the second
movement with its calm pace of a funeral march. Beethoven's
music seemed to him to be an immense, unshakable desire
to affirm human existence. The extraordinary surge toward
life that finally triumphed over the fear of death was surely
in keeping with Rei's state of mind. He prepared to listen to
Alban Berg's music in the second half of the concert, through
the mediation of Lieutenant Kurokami's granddaughter. What
sort of sound would emerge from the encounter between the
violin's four strings and the bow's ribbon of horsehair, now
in the hands of the young violinist who'd been introduced to
music by Black God?

After a long intermission that merely amplified the antici-
pation in his heart, Rei returned to his seat.

"Are you all right?" asked Hélène.

"Yes," said Rei, feebly. Hélène heard only a short, barely
audible intake of breath, as if his affirmation had not caused
his vocal cords to vibrate at all.

At last Midori Yamazaki walked on stage, her left hand holding both the neck of her dark violin and the heel of her bow, pointing vertically upward. Applause filled the hall. Responding with a gracious, sparkling smile to all the attention focused on her, the musician went up to the first violin, shook his hand, then turned back to the audience with a deep bow. The conductor, who had stood back while Midori greeted the audience, went over to the podium and bowed slightly. When he turned to face the musicians, the applause ceased abruptly. Midori was not wearing a brightly colored gown, as was often the case for a soloist or a singer, but a sober black jacket and trousers that seemed to indicate her intention to blend into the body of the orchestra. Her shoulder-length hair was tied at the back of her neck with a red ribbon. Rei could feel his heart pounding—at any second it might burst out of his rib cage. Hélène became aware that her companion's breathing was quickening in a way that was not normal. "Are you all right?" she whispered again, taking his hand. Rei didn't answer but squeezed her hand.

The conductor raised both arms, looking to the back left at the harpist and the clarinetists directly across from him. After a few seconds of tense, drawn-out silence, his arms came down slowly. The violinist prepared to set her bow on the strings to join pianissimo, on the second bar, the opening of the concerto *To the Memory of an Angel*. The first notes resembled a moment of silence before the beginning of the piece, as if the soloist were proceeding with the preliminary tuning of her instrument. The fingers of Midori's left hand had not yet touched the strings. The open string arpeggios were supported by the arpeggios of the two clarinets and the harp. It was the violin's natural sounds that could be heard. Rei was seized with an inner trembling.

Very soon, the music set off on a great ocean of dissonance from which now and again there unexpectedly emerged, like clearings bathed in the first rays of the rising sun, short melodic passages or chord arpeggios that did not offend the ears of those accustomed to the music that had preceded the arrival of the twelve-tone technique. Rei and Hélène were familiar with *To the Memory of an Angel*. They knew the work had been composed in response to the shock caused by the untimely death from polio, at the age of eighteen, of Manon Gropius—the daughter of Alma Mahler and the architect Walter Gropius. On listening to the first movement, which Midori performed brilliantly, Rei felt he was witnessing the deceased girl's immaculate childhood. He even felt that, through the clarity that indicated a fundamental conflict between tonality and atonality, he could make out flashes of a child's life as she joyfully strolled and played, laughing without restraint, singing at the top of her lungs.

According to the program, the second movement, which had begun with an Allegro of rare vehemence, demonstrated the onset of illness and the inexorable march toward death. Midori Yamazaki's violin writhed in agony, contrasting with the lush expansiveness of the orchestra: the cellos suggested the dull threat occasioned by the first signs of the disease, the brass evoked the terrible power of the life-threatening ailment, the tympani announced the paroxysm of suffering taking possession of the young girl's body. The pizzicati, acrobatically executed by the violinist's left hand, were so many stabs of shooting pain. Suddenly a calm fell: this was the famous quotation from Bach's cantata *O Ewigkeit, du Donnerwort*, introduced by the violin, then taken up by the clarinets. From that moment on, the music slid very gently over a terrain of gradual appeasement, coming to a serene end, where the violin rose steadily from one note to the next toward infinity, vanishing into silence . . .

12
.

THE SILENCE LASTED A LONG TIME. NO ONE DARED DISTURB IT.

Someone, however, drained of emotion and patience, timidly clapped their hands.

Everyone else followed.

And then there was an endless avalanche of applause.

13

CHEERS ERUPTED. THEY INCREASED WHEN THE VIOLINIST, demonstrating her particular appreciation for the harpist, gifted her with the bouquet of flowers she had just received. The soloist disappeared for the fourth time offstage after acknowledging the audience's inexhaustible applause with multiple bows. The conductor followed.

Now that the tension had lifted, Rei and Hélène felt a sort of depletion. The crowd of spectators went wild, increasing their cries of "Bravo!"

At last the musician returned, alone, with a cordless microphone in hand. She began to speak. Her voice was clear. Very suddenly a great calm descended over the hall, and all noise dissipated instantly, like rainwater absorbed by arid soil.

"Thank you so much, all of you, for coming this evening. As a rule, at a concert, the musicians don't speak. If they speak, they do so through the music. But this evening is special. I would like, actually, to tell you about my violin, this wonderful instrument on which I played Alban Berg's concerto *To the Memory of an Angel* this evening."

"Did you know it was yours?" asked Hélène.

"Yes. When she came on stage with her violin I wasn't sure . . . despite its unusual color. But from the first notes I knew it was my Vuillaume with your bow."

"This violin has been lent to me by a French luthier, Monsieur Jacques Maillard. He is Japanese as well. His name is Rei Mizusawa."

Midori was speaking slowly, her accent more American than Japanese.

"This violin was made by Nicolas François Vuillaume in 1857; he was the younger brother of the great Jean-Baptiste Vuillaume. It belonged to Monsieur Maillard's father, Yu Mizusawa. One day in 1938, the violin was destroyed, through an act of unthinkable violence."

Midori Yamazaki began to tell the story of Yu Mizusawa's violin.

"Forgive me, I'm not very comfortable speaking French. Excuse me while I read a little text I prepared for the occasion."

Midori took a sheet of paper from her inner jacket pocket and unfolded it. In the hall a deep silence reigned, comparable to that inside a great Zen temple in Kyoto.

14.

MIDORI WENT ON READING, LOOKING UP FROM THE WHITE SHEET of paper now and again.

"That little boy trembling with fear inside the wardrobe, who received his father's broken violin from my grandfather's hands, went on to become a luthier and devoted his life to restoring that violin. It is on that very instrument that I have had the honor of playing for you this evening, with a bow manufactured by his wife, Hélène Becker. I have found it to be an absolutely wonderful violin, comparable in every way to a Stradivarius or a Guarnerius. In any case, I have been completely won over by this Vuillaume-Maillard. I would even say that Nicolas François Vuillaume's original violin has been revived, improved, enriched, and enhanced by Jacques Maillard."

The violinist had stopped looking at her notes.

"Jacques Maillard is here among us this evening, with Hélène. I can see them from here. I cannot resist the pleasure of introducing them to you . . . Monsieur and Madame Maillard!"

Jacques and Hélène, surprised and disconcerted by this sudden attention, stood up and awkwardly submitted to the gazes of the spectators in the Salle Pleyel, who gave them a long ovation until, timidly, Midori motioned for silence.

"The evening is not yet over. Because I would like to play two pieces for you as an encore."

There was a storm of cheers and applause. The violinist waited. Silence returned, and she told the audience that she would like to play, first of all, the music that little Jacques had heard that day, before the soldiers arrived, and then the melody he had listened to so carefully from the solitary, terrifying darkness of the wardrobe. Midori explained that the first encore would be the first movement of Schubert's string quartet, *Rosamunde*.

"It is this masterpiece by Schubert that Monsieur Maillard's father, Yu Mizusawa, was rehearsing with his three Chinese friends. My grandfather was not there for the rehearsal, as you will have understood from my story. But Yu Mizusawa went on to tell him that the amateur musicians had been practicing this piece. I have an indelible memory of my grandfather tirelessly listening to this quartet. It was practically an obsession for him . . . And now I know why."

Four chairs had been set out in a semicircle at the front of the stage. Midori Yamazaki had consulted with three members of the orchestra to play the quartet. She would play first violin, Yu Mizusawa's role and place; Ghaleb Cheikh, violin; Joëlle Christophe, viola; and Jian Zhang, cello, would join her for the occasion.

"Here, then, is the first movement of Schubert's *Rosamunde* quartet."

While the three musicians from the orchestra moved to stand behind their chairs, Midori Yamazaki placed the microphone on the podium and, in turn, took her place. They greeted the audience, who, delighted by the Japanese violinist's singular proposal, applauded enthusiastically.

The four musicians sat down and tuned their instruments. Midori's violin, the Vuillaume-Maillard, gleaming with a dark shine, stood out from the other instruments, which were lighter in hue, more golden-orange. The two thousand spectators held their breath. The slightest rustle of clothing, the faintest creaking of a seat could be irksome. You could almost hear your neighbor breathing. Everyone anticipated the birth of Schubert's opening notes, which came from far away that night, very far, from another world, or perhaps even the other world, from a time and a place that were infinitely distant—a childhood slain, a torn, ancient memory, fractured and mutilated.

Finally, after the first two bars, with their obscure lapping of stagnant water, Midori's violin, marshaling around its soul at least three others—Yu Mizusawa's, Lieutenant Kurokami's, and Rei Mizusawa's—entered delicately, pianissimo, into Schubert's broad, deep melancholy.

In the near-impenetrable darkness of the huge Salle Pleyel, the Tokyo meeting room of 1938 emerged like a ghost, harboring the massive wardrobe where the little boy had sought refuge.

Rei went deeper into the darkness. A shiver ran down his spine.

15

·

MIDORI YAMAZAKI WAS THANKING THE THREE MUSICIANS FROM the orchestra who had kindly agreed to collaborate with her, shaking their hands, giving little nods again and again. After a moment she picked up the microphone she'd left on the podium and, with an understated gesture, tried to subdue the endless barrage of praise.

"Thank you. It is time now for the second piece. This is the little piece by Johann Sebastian Bach, the Gavotte en rondeau from the Third Partita for Solo Violin. Why the Gavotte en rondeau? Because this was what Monsieur Maillard's father performed that day in the presence of my grandfather, when he asked him to play."

Rei had removed his glasses, pressing the fingers of his left hand against his closed eyes. Hélène delicately placed her right hand on her partner's knee.

"I would like to dedicate this musical moment to the souls of Yu Mizusawa and Kengo Kurokami."

There was a burst of applause, which subsided quickly. A heavy silence fell over the hall.

Midori, with her arms by her sides, was holding the violin by the neck with her left hand, and in her right hand the heel of her bow. She closed her eyes. Her silent contemplation lasted over a minute. For the violinist it echoed the minute of silence she observed every year on August 6 at eight fifteen in the morning, thinking about the victims of Hiroshima, her grand-father's family, all exterminated, her grandfather himself who had *shamefully* survived the horrors of war, the bombing of Tokyo on March 10, 1945, and the hell of the atomic blast. She opened her eyes, placed her dark violin onto her left shoulder and under her chin, and slowly raised her right arm to set the bow upon the strings.

The piece began with a buoyant theme—jovial, bright, an adolescent's accompaniment from town as he sets out one sunny morning to walk through the countryside, driven by his happiness to be alive, stirred by his eagerness to explore the beauty of the surrounding landscape. At a certain point the music turned somber, as if conveying his apprehension on suddenly seeing a black mass of cloud on the horizon, which had been clear and radiant only minutes earlier. But it was only a fleeting darkness. Not long thereafter the cheer of the initial theme resurfaced. How many times had they already heard it, this smiling, sparkling motif? What was obvious, in its insistent reoccurrence, in this desire to endlessly *embroider* it, was the composer's unwavering devotion to its jolly little melody, like the unconditional affection felt for a simple child-hood tune that still resonates deeply, uninterrupted, like an inexhaustible spring, ready to gush forth at any second, from early youth to advanced age.

When, to conclude, the music returned for the fifth time to its initial theme, then slowed significantly to mark the end, Rei was overcome by a strange sensation that released him from the frozen space-time of his childhood, allowing him to land, at last, in the space-time of the present with Hélène and those they were close to. With the final notes, the violinist raised her right arm very slowly toward the ceiling.

A burst of cheers and applause came from all sides. The luthier raised his head to look at Midori, who bowed deeply. He was in a state of such mental and emotional agitation that he couldn't speak or make the slightest gesture. All he could do was turn to Hélène, who had just finished clapping energetically and was reaching for a tissue in her bag.

For a long time the entire audience remained as if transported to a degree rarely seen. Midori Yamazaki came and went, on and off the stage, taking numerous curtain calls. The musicians of the orchestra began to disperse. When Midori returned for the last time to thank the audience, only three or four people were left on stage. It was then that Rei noticed, at the back, very near the harp they were preparing to put away, a man in his fifties wearing a simple gray jacket, seated on the floor behind the empty chairs of the violin section. He was looking straight ahead, his eyes raised slightly toward the seats in the upper gallery. The man stood up. Then he began walking stage left. He turned his head from time to time toward the hall, his steps unsteady, like an old man or a hospital patient wheeling an IV pole. Rei sat up straight and leaned forward as he pushed his glasses onto his nose. Swallowing his saliva, he whispered, "Otōsan."

16

HÉLÈNE, SITTING NEXT TO JACQUES, HEARD HIM MURMUR A word she didn't know.

"What did you say?"

"No, it's nothing," said Jacques, turning his head to look at her. "Huh! He's not there anymore—he's vanished."

"Who?"

"My father, he was there, just now, *Otōsan* . . ."

EPILOGUE

1
.

THE DAY AFTER THE CONCERT, REI AND HÉLÈNE WENT TO SEE Midori and her mother. They had arranged to meet in the lobby of their hotel at five thirty in the afternoon. Rei and Hélène sat down on a sofa, waiting for Midori and Ayako to join them. A few minutes after the time set for the appointment, the two Japanese women arrived. Rei introduced Hélène to them. Hélène thanked the violinist for the *magnificent* concert and, above all, her kind consideration in honoring Jacques's work and her own. They had an aperitif together in the bar in the middle of the lobby. Each had a glass of champagne to celebrate the success of the concert and the exceptional event it represented in Rei's life and in Midori's.

"To your health!" said Hélène.

"To your health!" Ayako echoed timidly, in French.

"To the soul of Lieutenant Kurokami and the soul of my father."

"To the reborn soul of the Vuillaume-Maillard, or Vuillaume-Mizusawa, which reunited here tonight two souls that were once in communion long ago, and reunited all of us!" said Midori in turn.

They clinked glasses. Rei and Midori toasted each other a second time before taking a first sip of champagne. The conversation was mainly in French, but Rei also spoke Japanese, so that Ayako would not feel left out.

"Thank you, from the bottom of my heart, for this concert. I was deeply moved, as you can imagine. When did you decide you would use my father's violin?"

"As soon as the concert was programmed. That is, a year and a half ago. I really love your violin, you know. Ever since you left it with me, I've been ignoring my Strad a bit. I nearly always perform with yours."

"I'm very honored. I think your grandfather and my father were both there last night: during the two encores you played, of course, but also in your choice of the Berg concerto that your grandfather hoped you would play someday."

"That's true, it's something he said to me more than once. I think in Berg's music he could hear not only Manon Gropius's suffering, but also the suffering of the entire era when it was composed. To play *To the Memory of an Angel* was a way for me to remember your father's time and my grandfather's. All those very difficult years."

"The music that came from your violin was music that could wake the dead," added Hélène, who'd been listening to the conversation between Jacques and Midori as it alternated between French and Japanese.

"Wake the dead?" said Midori.

She turned to her mother to translate what she had just heard.

"Yes, the music was so *embodied* that it possessed the power to call souls back from the realm of the dead," said Hélène, looking at her companion.

"Indeed, last night, I thought I saw my father . . . I really *did* see my father."

Rei insisted on the word *did*, and went on to translate for Ayako what he had just said to her daughter.

"He was there, after the musicians had left, sitting on the floor behind the first violins' chairs."

The spring night was slowly falling. Their glasses were empty, except for Ayako's. Rei suggested they go to dinner.

"I've booked a table, not far from here. We can go on foot."

They got up.

The luthier placed his right hand on the violinist's shoulder.

"You must keep the violin forever. It needs you."

"With Hélène's bow?"

"Yes, of course," said the bow maker.

Then, squeezing her companion's left arm, as if a certain modesty prevented her from kissing him in public, Hélène continued: "This violin is his *father*. But at the same time his *child*. Today was his son's wedding day, or his daughter's. He will be parting from him, or her, for good . . . by entrusting the violin to you. I think it's a happy event for him, and for us. At last Jacques-Rei is entering another period in his life."

Jacques turned to face Hélène and kissed her tenderly on the brow.

2.

THERE WERE SEVERAL ARTICLES IN THE PRESS ABOUT MIDORI
Yamazaki's concert. Her brilliant, luminous performance of
the Alban Berg concerto and the two encores, along with the
extraordinary story she had told, attracted a wider audience
to appreciate the talented violinist, one that far surpassed the
limited circle of music lovers alone. But news of the concert
also shone a spotlight on the French-Japanese luthier Jacques
Maillard–Rei Mizusawa.

He was contacted by several journalists, including one,
notably, from the famous monthly journal *Music and Words*,
who offered to do a feature on him. Jacques agreed to meet the
journalist, Marcel Gaudin, who came to the luthier's workshop
three days in succession. Each interview lasted roughly two
hours. In addition to using a digital recorder, the journalist
took notes. In response to his questions, Jacques Maillard told
the entire story of Yu Mizusawa's violin. To conclude, the
conversation turned to the mysterious person who had been
on the empty stage after Midori's concert in Paris.

"So you saw your father."

"Yes. He looked tired, but he was just the way he'd been
sixty-seven years ago . . . wearing the same clothes. Midori
Yamazaki's music reached a dead man and brought him back

to me. Yes, he was a *revenant*, returned from the dead. These things happen, you know."

There was a long pause while the two men considered these words.

"Thank you for this long and fascinating interview. I'll try to put together a portrait that will focus on the *resurrection* of the violin."

Jacques got the impression that Marcel Gaudin emphasized the word *resurrection*.

"Do as you think best. You have my trust."

"Thank you. I'll send you the text when it's finished. You'll tell me what you think. Before I submit the final version, I'll take into account any comments or suggestions you might have . . ."

"Fine. That's perfect."

Two weeks later Jacques received a long five-page article titled "Fractured Soul: The Extraordinary Journey of a French-Japanese Luthier." Beneath the headline were photographs taken by the journalist: one of the interviewee in his work apron and one of his workshop. In the middle of the second page, filling the space of three narrow columns, was a photograph of Nicolas François Vuillaume's violin that Jacques had taken just after finishing the restoration on November 11, 1982, forty-four years after the soldier's efforts to destroy it.

Jacques took the liberty of correcting a few factual errors and two or three turns of phrase he thought didn't concord with his feeling of timid modesty, which never left him. He let a night go by. He reread the article three times. On the third reading he found a few more minute details that irked him. He forced himself to read it yet again and finally decided to send it back to Marcel Gaudin, thanking him for having finalized their long conversation.

Three weeks passed. Rei did not give the article in *Music and Words* another thought. He didn't see the time go by because, during those three weeks, he was devoting his energies—not as a luthier but as a translator—to the completion of a translation he'd begun years earlier, of Genzaburo Yoshino's *How Do You Live?*

3
·

THREE FATHER (OR PARENTAL) FIGURES HAD MOORED REI Mizusawa to life, to say nothing of Philippe and Isabelle Maillard, who had rescued him from the hell of war and his condition as a war orphan. First of all, there was Nicolas François Vuillaume's violin, which became the backbone of his life as a luthier and of his life, period; then there was Genzaburo Yoshino's book, which had *spoken* to him, constantly, from the place of an absent father. This explained his decision to devote himself *also* to the *resuscitation* of his father's voice through translation.

But what was the third element of the father figure? The ruined violin and Yoshino's book were the only things he'd been able to salvage from his life in Japan, cruelly and violently interrupted one day in November 1938. Since then, they had always been there—before him, with him, inside him— throughout his daily life in France. Many years later, when he was already an old man, the pink cardigan and the novel by Takiji Kobayashi were added to his personal collection of mementos that had witnessed his lost past. But these last two items could hardly be said to have escorted him through his long years of development.

Unlike his father's violin or Yoshino's book, there was something that could not be preserved, much to Rei's despair.

In fact, it wasn't a thing but a living creature: the Shiba Inu
that had so mysteriously appeared that Sunday, as night was
falling, on the path of his solitary walk home. Philippe and
Isabelle, his adoptive parents, had agreed to let Rei keep the
animal for the short span of time they remained in the Japanese capital. But the day Rei, with his French parents, left Japan
behind for good, he'd had to part with the dog he'd baptized
Momo. The dog had been entrusted to one of the Maillards'
neighbors. It was a wrenching experience for Rei. In his struggle
against a crumbling world, Rei had eventually concluded that,
conversely to the stork in the famous tale that was transformed
into a beautiful woman to thank the man that rescued it, his
father, who could no longer appear before him as his father,
had decided to slip into the guise of Momo. And yet, in leaving
Momo behind, he'd had to part from his father a second time.
Rei's heart was broken. Philippe and Isabelle knew how deep
and painful the boy's wound must be—that it would be open
and bleeding and raw for a very long time. How could they
dress such an unhealable wound? How could they make it
less piercing? They came up with the idea of giving the son of
Yu Mizusawa, who was now their own, a puppy from a litter
belonging to Isabelle's sister's family. This dog, also called
Momo, stayed with Rei through his entire adolescence. The
dog was very old, nearing his final days, when the young
man began his apprenticeship as a luthier in Mirecourt. It was
only many years later, once he had put the finishing touches
to restoring his father's violin, that Rei allowed himself to
be tempted by the company of another dog. An opportunity
arose for him to adopt a Shiba. He could not resist the urge

to live with it. Nor could he conceive of any other name than Momo. In fact, so far as Rei was concerned, every dog on the planet was named Momo, whether male or female, just as to him every violin on the planet was a cousin or even a brother of the Nicolas François Vuillaume.

By the time Jacques Maillard was going over the proofs of the article for *Music and Words* and working hard on his translation of Genzaburo Yoshino, he was on his fourth Momo.

4.

AT LAST, THE INTERVIEW "FRACTURED SOUL: THE EXTRAORDI-nary Journey of a Japanese-French Luthier" was published. Rei read it in one sitting. Quite naturally, the idea came to him to translate the words he'd shared with Marcel Gaudin into Japanese, in order to send the article to Lin Yanfen in Shanghai. It took him a whole week to do it. He immediately sent Yanfen's great-nephew the Japanese text, along with a letter describing Midori's concert in Paris. Over ten months had passed since his visit to the hospital in Shanghai. When he'd received the message from Midori Yamazaki announcing her concert at the Salle Pleyel, he'd immediately written to Yanfen to share his silent joy at the prospect of being able to hear Lieutenant Kurokami's granddaughter perform. Yanfen's reply had been laconic: "I'm glad for you, that you'll have this opportunity to find your Black God again."

Three days later, Rei got a message from Yanfen's great-nephew confirming that he'd received the article. The message was reduced to a bare minimum.

Then, silence.

A silence that lasted roughly two weeks.

One day, when the article in *Music and Words* had practically retreated from the luthier's recent memory, an envelope arrived for him from China.

It was a letter from Yanfen, on two sheets of pale pink A4 paper, written using Word.

May 17, 2005
Shanghai Municipal Hospital

Dear Rei-san,
You cannot imagine the joy I felt on reading "Fractured Soul: The Extraordinary Journey of a French-Japanese Luthier." Thank you for translating it for me.

Your visit to the hospital filled me with joy. It made it possible for me to do something I had to do before leaving this earth: return the pink cardigan and Takiji Kobayashi's book to you. If I couldn't have done that, I would have been filled with remorse. My soul—if you'll pardon me the expression—would have stayed nailed forever to a rough wall of the here-below, like a kite trapped in thick foliage.

Reading the article in *Music and Words* gave me the opportunity to reflect on everything you told me during that unforgettable day we spent together in my hospital room. In so doing, you gave me a wonderful opportunity to follow you through each stage of your career as a luthier, as it took shape around Yu's violin. You lost your father that day, on November 6, 1938, in tragic circumstances, but when all is said and done, you always lived with him through his violin, which you still had thanks to Lieutenant Black God.

With your description of Midori Yamazaki's concert in

Paris you made it possible for me to attend that historic event in my mind, and through the magic of music it united the three main protagonists of the story! I thank you, Rei-san, for the thoughtful consideration that drove you to share the minute details of the evening with me. I am quite prepared to believe what you wrote about Yu, that he *came back*, summoned by the sound of his violin, and that he departed again once he'd heard the two encores that embodied him. His soul was attached, somewhere, to the roof of a house, to the branch of a tree or the step of a stone staircase; he had come, no doubt, to look for it . . . Lieutenant Black God, too, was called back by Johann Sebastian Bach's Gavotte en rondeau, as well as Alban Berg's *To the Memory of an Angel*. He was probably there. I like to think that Yu and Black God met each other again on that occasion, after so many years of deathly silence. Berg composed that absolutely heartbreaking music in 1935, in other words only three years before the catastrophe struck us. We didn't know, of course. The suffering contained in that work and the near silent prayer that gradually emerges from it by the end are perhaps the very signatures left by *our* era . . . I wonder if it wasn't just such a thought that troubled the heart of Black God.

Modern medicine has shown what it is capable of by unexpectedly prolonging my life. My attending physician is the first to be surprised. But medicine has its limits, because this time I think I really am reaching the end of my days. I am writing this letter to you once again through the help of my devoted great-nephew, but I think it will be the last one I will ever write. I am leaving you, my dearest Rei-san. My life, which I wish had been different from the one allotted me, is reaching its end. It is a deliverance, mingled with infinite regrets. For those of us who are staring death in the face, it is a painful experience. But my dying is a painful moment softened by consolation, a consolation that has come, to be sure, rather late. But it is real, and it is what your miraculous reappearance did for my long lifeless life, which I had thought irremediably ruined by Yu's sudden and brutal disappearance. I felt connected to him, even if in all likelihood he did not realize it. That is why I am glad it occurred to me to start searching for a trace of your life, and that I decided to write you. My last days have been brightened by your presence, and you gave Yu back to me in telling me the story of how you resuscitated his violin. Until then, the only memory I had of it was of a tortured thing, a mournful image.

You will find enclosed two little photographs I've kept carefully over the years. The first is of our Sino-Japanese quartet. It was taken the day of our first rehearsal of *Rosamunde*, the day we founded the quartet. Your father, first violin, was the oldest of the four; he's on the far left. You can see him with his Nicolas François Vuillaume. In the second photograph, you can see me together with your father. Cheng, the cellist, took the picture the day Yu lent me the pink cardigan. I am wearing it—do you recognize it?

I might have given them to you when you came to the hospital, but I couldn't. My natural shyness prevented me from doing so spontaneously. But now that I know it's the last and only chance I have to send them to you, I can do it openly and without hesitation. They could have burned with me in my coffin, but I dare to believe, rather, that they might find a place among the documents of your life . . .

I will leave you now, dear Rei-san, with the boundless sorrow I have felt in my soul for so long—not dissimilar, in essence, to the sorrow expressed in Schubert's *Rosamunde*.

さようなら. そしてもう一度, ありがとう. Farewell, and once again, thank you.

林硯芬 Lin Yanfen

The last line, as well as Lin Yanfen's last and first name, was written in blue ink, in fine, if slightly trembling, cursive handwriting, the hand of the author herself.

At dawn exactly eight days after receiving this letter, Rei got a short email message from Yanfen's great-nephew informing him of his great-aunt's death. She had passed on during the night a few hours earlier, alone, without anyone noticing.

That same day Jacques Maillard had been notified that the reading committee of a major publishing house had agreed to publish his translation of *How Do You Live?*

5
.

IT WAS TEN O'CLOCK IN THE MORNING. REI WAS SEATED IN THE armchair of the little sitting area, resting and drinking a coffee. He had the publisher's letter in hand. All of a sudden, he got up and went to the living room.

Taking off his navy-blue apron, he tossed it onto the sofa. He opened the door to the cupboard where they kept the pictures and memories of loved ones who had died, long ago or recently, people who had never been forgotten but were still present: his father, his mother, a few master luthiers from Mirecourt and Cremona, Philippe and Isabelle Maillard, Momo I, Momo II, Momo III, Lieutenant Kurokami the "Black God," and Lin Yanfen. It was an altar, indeed, a real altar, but an altar that did not come under the sway of any sort of worship. Jacques Maillard, or Rei Mizusawa, was a man without religion. He did not believe in any sort of afterlife. What would remain at the very end, the end of everything, of civilization, humanity, the planet, the solar system? Everything would be engulfed, forgotten, lost. When all was said and done, wouldn't life be a gigantic hecatomb? Why go on adding to it? Why commit the abysmal folly of propagating still more death—the death that war generates, ruthlessly, in the trenches, in the camps, with bombs raining down to tear you apart, the death caused by weapons of mass destruction, all the way to the atom bomb, burning and reducing entire cities to ash in less than an instant, raising a hideous, diabolic mushroom cloud in the sky after the sudden, blinding deflagration of satanic light? Why so much cruelty? Why so many atrocious, murderous acts? And yet, that was just it: because of these unbelievable acts of violence, this irremissible slaughter that brutally precluded life and which, by that very fact, gave rise to an interminable procession of ghosts, the creation of an altar had become absolutely necessary for Rei Mizusawa. It was an altar that, first and foremost, restored his murdered father to him, and then all the dead who were with him, near or far. That being the case, his art as a luthier, his art of rendering "the sounds of the soul," of inner life, of darkest melancholy as of deepest joy—thanks to composers living or dead and the mediation of peerless performers—through the instruments he created, after so many years of apprenticeship, of trial and error, hesitation, research, after so much effort invested in the patient and passionate study of the old masters' great models, after, above all, an entire life, which was moreover fairly ordinary, spent in the company of his father's violin, repairing, restoring, maintaining . . . his art, therefore, devoted entirely to the service of human emotion, was nothing more than the attempt to ease the traumatic pain caused by the devastating destruction of that which binds you most firmly to the world and to life.

At the very back of the shelf in the cupboard, the pink cardigan could be seen, carefully folded inside a transparent plastic bag, next to the ancient copy of *The Crab Cannery Ship*, which leaned against the side of the cupboard, dog-eared, yellowed, and considerably worn by the weight of years. Kengo Kurokami's cardboard memorial acted as a stand for the two small, yellowed photographs Rei had received from Yanfen eight days earlier. Next to them Rei had placed a photograph of the elderly Chinese woman, trying to smile as she leaned against the mattress of her bed, the head of which had been elevated almost vertically, a photograph he had taken when he visited her at the hospital in Shanghai. Finally, at the front of the shelf, a very recent color photograph of the Vuillaume-Mizusawa-Maillard violin had been placed on a tiny easel.

Hands together, I am standing straight as an ancestral cypress before the strange little community of the dead. With a firm, determined gesture, I insert the publisher's letter, folded in four, inside the pages of Takiji Kobayashi's book. Hélène is here, discreet, by my side or rather behind me to my right, standing back. Can she see my lips moving? I murmur a few inarticulate words which I'm sure she cannot hear. After such a long moment of contemplation, I close the door to the cupboard.

I slowly put my navy-blue apron back on. I vanish into the half-light of my workshop, my arm around Hélène's waist.

ACKNOWLEDGMENTS

Contrary to expectation, it was during the planning phase of my text "Shindemo shinikirenai," which was published in the anthology *Armistice* (Gallimard, 2018), edited by Jean-Marie Laclavetine, that the idea for *Fractured Soul* came to me, and it took shape at such a dazzling pace that I myself was astonished. As I get older I have begun to feel, whether it's in Tokyo where I live, or in Hiroshima where I put the finishing touches on "Shindemo shinikirenai," that we are surrounded by ghosts, the living dead, who are lost in the space of the between-the-two-deaths. Quite naturally, therefore, it is to Jean-Marie that my initial thanks must go. If he had not dared to invite me to contribute to *Armistice*, and if, moreover, I had not felt so lighthearted that I immediately responded with a comfortable, carefree yes, this novel in all likelihood would never have seen the light of day.

A NOTE FROM THE TRANSLATOR

I've always been wary of titles. At first glance, Akira Mizubayashi's *Âme brisée* did not seem particularly treacherous or
demanding. Two words, a noun and its adjective; the English
equivalent springs easily to mind: fractured or broken soul.

But when I read the very first page—the epigraph page, in
fact—the novel's short, obvious title suddenly loomed above
me with all its significance and innuendo, in what is ostensibly
a dictionary entry:

> Âme, subst. fém. *Musique. Âme d'un instrument à cordes.*
> Petite pièce de bois interposée, dans le corps de l'instru-
> ment, entre la table et le fond, les maintenant à la bonne
> distance et assurant la qualité, la propagation comme
> l'uniformité des vibrations.

> *Trésor de la langue française*

I discovered, to my delight and horror, that the word *âme*,
in addition to being the French equivalent of our own word for
soul, signifying the spirit or emotional sense of identity, as some
dictionaries define it, is also used in French to designate a very
specific small piece of wood found in stringed instruments such

as violins, violas, and cellos: a wooden peg that is in fact, in its own way, the soul of the instrument, the tiny material element that gives beauty and heart to the sound produced by the bow against the strings. Its position inside the instrument is crucial, as is its condition. If anything happens to it, the sound deteriorates, the music loses beauty and harmony, and the instrument must be repaired.

Obviously, this was my first encounter with the terminology of instrument making; I have never played the violin and only played the piano very hopelessly for five years. And my initial reaction, as translator, was mild panic. It seemed unlikely to me that in English the word *soul* would also be part of a violin. I have often rued the rather too-practical or business-like nature of English, ever since I first bought a commercial salt shaker in Greece that was marked, in Greek, *To Alati tis Zois* (The Salt of Life), and in English, Table Salt for all Domestic Purposes. I feared for Mr. Mizubayashi's use of *âme*, with its beautiful double meaning: the broken soul of the human protagonist occupies most of the story, as does the broken violin.

On checking my usual bilingual dictionary, I found the basic word in English for the *âme* of a stringed instrument is a "sound post." As I feared, a descriptive word for what the little piece of wood is, and what it does, on a purely practical, material basis. *Broken* or *Fractured Sound Post* would hardly be a fitting title for anything but a luthier's instruction manual. In desperation I began to dig further. I had received my translation degree a few years before word processors and the internet; we learned how to research at libraries, with infinite patience and copious note-taking. Would I, without the internet, have unearthed the necessary information I did not yet know I needed to find?

Fortunately, my panic was short-lived. Several online sources about violin manufacture informed me that an alternative name for the sound post was soul post or even *âme*. I imagined a small cohort of Anglophone luthiers, or musicians, convening to defend the esthetic and spiritual nature of their respective professions, out of respect, perhaps, for their fellows in Cremona or Mirecourt, or on concert stages from Tokyo to Paris.

I eventually decided to "invent" a dictionary entry for a fictitious *Treasures of the English Language* modeled on the French epigraph, where I could happily show the common name for the *âme* alongside its more evocative, occasional appellation.

SOUND POST or SOUL POST, noun. *Music. The sound post of a stringed instrument.* Little wooden dowel inserted into the body of the instrument, between the top plate and back plate, to maintain them at the proper distance and ensure the quality, resonance, and uniformity of the vibrations.

Treasures of the English Language

I was still faced with a lesser dilemma: Which word would I use when Jacques the luthier is in his workshop? Soul post—less common, possibly unknown even to some violinists—or sound post, the accepted technical term?

In the end, I decided that Midori Yamazaki's Stradivarius or the violins being repaired by Jacques Maillard would have sound posts; only Yu Mizusawa's violin, in this novel, has a soul post. Perhaps an arbitrary translator's choice, a half measure to rescue a significant word from its potential loss in translation; I can only hope that Akira Mizubayashi will approve, and his readers understand.

Here ends Akira Mizubayashi's
Fractured Soul.

The first edition of the book was printed and
bound at Lakeside Book Company in
Harrisonburg, Virginia, March 2023.

A NOTE ON THE TYPE

The text of this novel was set in Palatino, an old-style serif designed in the late 1940s by Hermann Zapf and named after the sixteenth-century Italian calligrapher. Zapf set out to craft a Renaissance-inspired typeface whose legibility could overcome the shortcomings—including poor quality paper—of printing in his native Germany at the time. Achieving this through its width, thickened weight, and larger proportions, Palatino renders text in startling clarity, distinguishing it as one of the most readable and popular book types today.

HARPERVIA

An imprint dedicated to publishing international voices,
offering readers a chance to encounter other lives and other
points of view via the language of the imagination.